THE
DEVIL
TO
PAY

A THRILLER BY
KIT BERLIN

Published in Canada by Engen Books, St. John's, NL.

Library and Archives Canada Cataloguing in Publication

Title: The devil to pay / a thriller by Kit Berlin.
Names: Berlin, Kit, author.
Identifiers: Canadiana (print) 20210127074 | Canadiana (ebook) 20210127147 |
ISBN 9781774780183
  (softcover) | ISBN 9781774780190 (PDF)
Classification: LCC PS8603.E689 D38 2021 | DDC C813/.6—dc23

This book is a work of fiction. Names, characters, places and incidents are
products of the author's imagination or are used fictitiously. Any resemblance
to actual events or locales or persons living or dead is entirely coincidental.

Distributed by:
Engen Books
www.engenbooks.com
submissions@engenbooks.com

First mass market paperback printing: April 2021

Cover Image: Ellen Curtis

THE DEVIL TO PAY

A THRILLER BY
KIT BERLIN

ENGEN
BOOKS

Vivien Ellis pulled open the Velcro closures of her body armour.

"Recommending against this Inspector Ellis. Strongly against," said Sergeant Neary. "Superintendent is on the way. Wait."

"Bullet proof top doesn't look very conciliatory, Sergeant Neary." Vivien handed Neary the Kevlar vest, its five pounds feeling heavier in the hand than over the shoulders.

Neary had a decade on Vivien and she outranked him. He was one of those cops more comfortable in a uniform than a suit. Neary had advanced as far as he could and that was as far as he ever wanted. The blue uniform was Neary's day-to-day body armour, his costume saying *cop*.

Funny the things that came into your head under stress.

Vivien let her hair out, allowing the neglected auburn mane to fall over her shoulders, guessing this might also make her look less threatening. She undid her belt, on which her sidearm, a SIG Sauer P286, was holstered, and handed that to Neary too. Strip poker. High stakes.

"The lad in the house, Maher, he's fuckin' nuts," Neary was pleading, "There is no indication you're welcome in there. Furlong and Warren have dealt with him in the past and say he's violent. He's unpredictable."

"He's holding a child hostage. I don't see the alternative," said Vivien. Though she did see, plainly, an alternative in the form of three SWAT team snipers in position, rifles aimed at the house, itching to pull their triggers. They could, if given the green light, wait until the suspect, Maher, stayed too long looking out a window and, with skill and some luck, blow his brains out. The kid inside would witness this and replay it in his head for the rest of his life. Bad enough what he would already be carrying with him without being sprayed by viscera from a successful head shot.

And the eager sniper too, he or she would wear the round they fired forever, would go suddenly or slowly mad from having extinguished the life of another human being.

"It isn't done, it is not protocol. You are freelancing," said Neary. "I'm going on record because there will be an inquisition. I am going on record."

"Good thing I'm the hostage negotiator and have rank," answered Vivien. "You're in the clear, Neary. I'll tell them you protested, that you were against it. I will make absolutely certain your objections are in all the reports."

The young man in the house holding the boy wasn't talking to anyone, hadn't responded at all. There was a landline inside and they'd called it, but he hadn't picked up. They were close enough, the walls of the house thin enough, that they could hear the phone ringing. They'd been hailing him via loudspeaker but he gave no acknowledgement of having heard that either. They knew he was still alive from glimpses of movement, the play of shadows, through gaps in the curtains. The condition of his hostage was unknown.

Vivien knew that Neary was right, that what she was doing was wrong, was unlikely to work. But fearing for the child's life…no, selfishly fearing of what she would have to live with for the rest of her own life if the child died…she was going to offer to exchange herself for the current captive. There was no indication the hostage-taker would agree to this, it was a desperate measure. Dying trying was, Vivien calculated, preferable to being haunted by the boy having been murdered, or worse, in there.

"Listen," said Neary, "Mark is on his way, at least discuss it with him first."

An entreaty she wait for guidance from her husband, a fellow Constabulary officer the same rank as herself, before making a rash decision? That settled it, she was going in.

She started her walk across the empty street toward the front door of the row house, her hands up, raised just above her shoulders, carrying no weapon, wearing no vest. Most of St. John's, Newfoundland burned to the ground in 1892 and the town was rebuilt in haste. The attached houses, painted in bright, even gaudy colours featured as an attraction in all the tourism ads, but in reality, those made for working people, like the one toward which she was walking, were simply balloon frames of dubious construction. A bird of some sort, a starling perhaps, emerged from a hole under the eave and flew away. There was a nest up there.

It was a fine summer day, she could feel the heat of the sun on her face, smell the lilacs that were coming into bloom in the yard of every second house in a neighbourhood of this age. The back of her shirt was damp with sweat from having worn the bullet proof vest and was now cool against her skin as the moisture evaporated.

She would do this job, free this boy, and—if she survived—she would quit policing. She thought now that her hair was a mess and she should have left it up. She was long overdue a visit to the salon. Another of the "things to do" if she lived.

"Gary!" she called out. "I'm coming down there. I want us to talk, Gary. I just want to talk."

Two Years later.
New Orleans, May 29, 2019

Someone, sometime since 1716, when the cabinet maker Thomas Hache of Grenoble crafted the desk, had cut three deep notches in that part of one leg (there were eight legs!) where the occupant's right hand naturally fell. It was an expensive piece the first time it sold and had, over its three hundred odd years, grown, steeply, in value. The desk's otherwise scrupulous care was seen to by every man who sat behind it. It had sustained no significant damage but for the triplet of scars in the one leg. Serious collectors were appalled its current owner, Gustave Polk, actually used the desk in business, believing it belonged in a museum. Three centuries and the only thing to mar the original maker's masterful effort was that discrete trio of confident gashes, three deep cuts made with a sharp blade and a steady hand.

What was so important that it merited being

scored three times in the walnut? Sexual conquests, Polk supposed. The birth of children? Kings and Queens to various thrones? And, from the way the wood had been smoothed away around the wounds, it was clear that all the previous owners, like Polk, could not resist running their fingers over them. The act was contemplative, like the rolling of prayer beads through the fingers, and Polk always found himself doing so as he listened with intent, as he was now to James Elgin, a younger man not long in his employ.

"These are firesale prices," said Elgin, sitting across the grand desk from Polk. "If you consider what these sorts of assets would have gone for not five years ago." They were considering the purchase of an offshore oil rig used for exploration and currently stationed, idle, in a small bay off Newfoundland, on Canada's eastern coast. Polk had become wealthy in the trade of such things, first in the Gulf of Mexico, its waters visible from his eleventh story office window, and then around the world. He specialized in finding assets of companies in financial distress and making only unreasonable offers he knew the sellers must accept.

"And move it where, Elgin? The downturn is global."

"West Africa? If it is a downturn."

"And not…?"

"The end of something."

Polk laughed.

"The end of oil? What have you been reading, Elgin?"

"I read everything, sir, paying particular attention to those authors with whom I am predisposed to disagree."

Polk clapped his hands thinking Elgin might have been his best hire in ages.

"Only greed makes a cartel. The Saudis and Iranians and Russians will all lay together in the same bed and the price will be set where shale oil and the tar sands are poison to the lenders. Or, alternatively, they grow apart and then one day a proxy of the House of Saud fires a missile into Tehran, the ensuing conflict closes the Gulf of Hormuz, the world supply is halved, and the price goes through the roof. This isn't an insight, Elgin, it is fact." Polk's fingers ran over the three cuts in the desk leg and for the first time thought that they might have been put there by the maker himself, by Hache, who foresaw the want of the physical aide to meditation. That would have been rare genius.

"Wind, solar…" said Elgin.

"When battery storage is magical. Not in my lifetime, and that is the period which most interests me."

"How long do you suppose the price will stay at a level…"

"There is at least a year's supply of oil on the waves so…"

Polk picked up some documents Elgin had provided. There were the usual technical specifications and the rig's history of maintenance but also a glossy sheet featuring several colour photographs. Polk held this up for Elgin to see. Elgin understood the gesture was meant as a query.

"It was attached, a fact sheet about Newfoundland, some promotional bumph."

Preparing to discard the sheet Polk gave it a cursory glance.

"I've been, you know, Elgin."

"To Newfoundland, sir?"

"Yes. You cannot photograph the wind." There was nothing Polk didn't already know in the pictures, a dramatic rocky landscape, quaint fishing villages, woolly Irish types sawing away at fiddles in pubs.

"So," Elgin asked, "the assets are stranded for three, four years minimum?"

But Polk could no longer hear his able assistant. His eye was drawn to a detail in the photo, taken in the public house, a detail that caused a deafening hum in Polk's ear. The musical yokels in the pub appeared to be sitting on an old church pew, the aisle end of which was decorated with a crudely sculpted mermaid, a particular sort of sea creature, with a beatific smile, bent just below the navel where her human form gave way to a fish's tail, so that it appeared she was sitting up on the water's surface and presenting, in her right hand, a primitive comb.

"...or do you see something on the demand side?" Elgin was finishing.

"I'll go straight away," said Polk, standing and then tugging his vest down, a sign that Elgin should rise and follow his orders without hesitation. Elgin stood, perplexed.

"To Newfoundland, sir?"

"Yes, tell Mrs. Guidry she is to call Leon at Lakefront to see that our plane is ready. Bob Gardner is my preference for a pilot. Bob can turn around and come back straight away as I am unsure how long I'll be there."

"We are buying this rig, Mr. Polk?"

"I really don't believe we will, Mr. Elgin. But there is something I need see for myself. Please see to my plane right away, I wish to leave today."

"Very well, sir."

Polk further adjusted his clothes, pulling down

his French cuffs to expose jeweled links by Jean Michel Schlumberger. Made in 1959 they were the newest Polk owned. Polk watched the door close behind Elgin and picked up the phone.

"Mrs. Guidry can you please put me through to Mr. Prum. Yes, Zurich Prum not Hamburg Prum. Thank You."

Clonfert, Ireland
519 AD

The blood and bowel running between his fingers was turning cold. The man was shaking uncontrollably and could not crawl or even drag himself further. The cries of his wife had ended suddenly so he supposed they had cut her neck or smashed in her skull. Those of his son faded as the boy had disappeared with the raiders, taken, he believed, as a slave. The thieving band were Deer People, Osraige, still unbaptised, refusing salvation. They'd probably been drawn here by the Monks' cattle. The flames from the burning village now threw enough light that he could see her smiling down at him from the wall of the church, comb in hand, blessed sea beast and so let himself succumb to the rough wound the sword had made in him. The Mermaid would take him up.

***

His confessor, bold and wise Breandán, had

warned the young monk the day would come when raiders would set upon the village and, being godless, would ransack the church. He was to take the treasured object from its sanctuary, put it in a fine leather purse, double knot its straps round his neck and run all the way to the sea where Breandán would always be waiting. He was to run for a night and a day without stopping, except to take small drinks of water. Other monks would stay behind to fight off any who hoped to find his trail. He had practiced running through the wood in darkness deeper than this. The moon and stars were as torches tonight. He was the fastest and the sturdiest of all the monks. Even as he knew those who had stayed behind were being slain, the righteousness of his deed lifted him. He went faster still, God within him.

The Banks of Newfoundland
519 AD

Breandán's head rolled and he saw that Brother Mael had perished in the night. The face and lips a raw red yesterday were white and blue in the dawn, his eyes, without light in them, looking to heaven. Breandán would unlash himself from the ox hide of the raft and say a blessing. Who would pray for the last monk among them to die? They were now twelve days on the waves and without food or freshwater for the last four. If his Brothers felt he had betrayed them they said nothing. And what of the holy relic that the gentle boy had conveyed from its keep in Clonfert, would it go to the bottom of this frigid ocean with him, would it be eaten by the fishes and so go back from whence it had come? Perhaps that was always God's will.

As his rough leather tethers became sodden with brine the more painfully they cut into his flesh and the harder they were to untie. Or was it merely that his flesh was growing weaker. The sea turtle they'd eaten might sustain them for another day or two, but they were all going mad from thirst. A whale, a leviathan, had breached near the raft yesterday, its vast back taking an age to roll through the surf, like a great mill stone turning beneath the waves. The day before that they had drifted past a towering island of ice, afloat on the waves. They could not navigate their raft close enough to harvest the frozen water, which one of the monks said was purported to be fresh. It was a terrible test of faith. All they could do was witness these wonders. There were no waves this morning, but the swells were long and deep. Freed from the ropes Breandán stood and grasped the mast to steady himself. It was judgement day. Spears were falling from the sky, piercing the water all around the boat, black lines shooting from the lead-coloured sky. No, these were birds, diving birds, coming back up out of the water with shimmering, quivering finger-length fish in their bills. The birds were raining down on the sea in the tens of thousands. Brother Eremon saw this too but was in such a weakened condition as to be unable to even react. Brother Labras too, he saw now had been received by his maker in the night. They were now three in number. Breandán squinted and saw, on the western horizon a dark bar. "Talamh!" he cried, pointing "Talamh." Land!

St. John's
May 30, 2019

Terry noted the disapproval on Mary's face the moment she spotted him from the door of the pub. He supposed he should have waited but he was parched. He checked and saw he had already demolished most of the pint of stout.

Mary pulled out a chair and sat as heavily as her small frame would allow.

"Are you crazy, Terry!"

"One pint."

"No, here! This place." She looked over the grim room. "Polk is one of the heaviest hitters in this game! We'll get crabs from these chairs."

"He chose it. He said this is where we were to meet. I suggested the hotel and he said, *The Sportsman.*"

Mary did an inventory of the place. One shelf behind the bar was dedicated to old, dented, dust-covered sporting trophies. A ledge over the door to the Mens provided a perch for some patchy taxidermy on what had probably been a fox but might just as well have been a stray mongrel, a crackie dog. The walls were mostly large wooden panels, no doubt once very grand but now heavy with an almost black, blue paint. Many of the tables had benches, sections cut from old church pews. It smelled of stale tobacco, despite the prohibition against doing so they likely smoked in here after the doors were locked for the night. The clientele were of that downtown St. John's tribe that fancied themselves artists, actors and painters and such but were, in the main, simple ne'er do wells and alcoholics. There could be no reason a man of wealth and refinement, like Gustave Polk, would want to meet in such a place. There was some mistake. Mary was wearing a fine skirt with a perfect fit and a new blouse purchased just for this meeting. She looked at Terry.

"Why are you dressed like that?" Terry was wearing a down vest with reflective Scotchlite striping over a heavy woolen shirt. He was in jeans and steel-toed construction boots.

"I came straight from the supply ship. Listen, he's in the oil business, he's seen people dressed like this. Maybe he's into traditional music or something."

"Please no, Terry. Anything but trad."

Mary glanced again at the bar. The place watered more than the bohemians, there were thieves and drug dealers here too. A hooligan at the rail caught her eye and sent a message of dangerous hunger within. It was no place for them to have a business meeting with stakes as high as these.

She knew Polk right away, the quality of fabric and cut of his suit was visible even with the light at his back as he came through the door. Mary stood. Polk seemed to be letting his eyes adjust to the darkness. Mary started to go to greet him when he spotted her, reasoned who she was and waved her back. He extended a hand.

"Ms. Hounsell?"

"Yes. Welcome to Newfoundland, Mr. Polk."

"I am surely delighted to be here, more so now that I've met you."

Mary smiled, not so much at the remark but at Polk's Louisiana accent, and the slightly higher pitch at which men from that part of the world spoke. There was bird song in his voice. Mary bid Terry stand. Terry put out his hand.

"And this is Terry Jedore," she said. "He knows everything there is to know about that rig."

"Today, put business aside. Let us first get acquainted?"

"Best practice," offered Terry.

"It is, it is," said Polk, "you two sit and let me buy you a drink. Ms. Hounsell?"

"Mary, please. I won't have the house white here so just an Irish whiskey on the rocks."

"Mr. Jedore?"

"A pint of Guinness, please."

Polk made for the bar, appearing perfectly unworried about the unsavoury characters leaning against it. He'd been around, Mary reasoned.

"Seems a nice fellow," said Terry.

***

"A double Irish Whiskey on the rocks, double vodka and soda and a pint of Guinness, please"

Gustave Polk surveyed the room. It bore little resemblance to the cozy, charming spot in the tourism promotional material he'd seen back in New Orleans. Whoever had taken those photographs had dressed and staged the place, brought in models with better diets and fewer habits than the regulars, photo-shopped out the dents and nicks, the scratches and mismatching patches. This did not surprise or disappoint Gustave Polk for now his eye fell upon the very church pew he'd seen on the glossy page, roughly hewn and decorated with an almost hypnotically charming, if rudimentary, carving of the mermaid of Clonfert. It was all Polk could do to stay where he was, leaning against the bar and not rush to the pew, get down on his knees and examine the carving of the sea monster clutching a comb.

"Twenty-two fifty" the barmaid's words turned Polk's head. She was a raven-haired woman, in her thirties, Polk supposed. The Guinness was well-poured, a modest overflow of the creamy head running down the glass was wiped clean. The glass holding his vodka was spotted from having not gotten similar attention when plucked from the dishwasher.

Polk handed over two Canadian twenties.

"Are those church pews?" he asked the barmaid.

"Yes, and I believe the wood panel on the walls came from the same place. De...whatcha call it. When they close a church?"

"Deconsecrated?"

"Das it," she said and laughed showing she was missing a tooth.

"Which church, do you know?" asked Polk.

"Hank?" the barmaid called to a derelict man seated down the bar. "What was the name of that church that Jack got the pews and the panelling out of?"

"Up the shore, in Ferryland," Hank said, his eyes fixed on his beer. "St. Brendan's."

Polk nodded. Yes, St. Brendan's, of course. He left a five-dollar tip and picked the drinks from the bar. "Thank you," he said.

June 2, 2019

Pouring himself a drink the Archbishop looked down to see he had ruined yet another cardigan with his smoking. He took precautions, was mindful of the cigarette ash but clearly tiny bits of the burning end fell to his protruding belly and burnt tiny holes, invisible to his ageing eyes, which then grew in the wool as it was stretched or laundered. He was in his rights to smoke, but he knew it was generally frowned upon these days, so The Most Reverend Archbishop Aiden Patrick Doyle kept the habit, as much as possible, to himself. He endeavoured never to smell of cigarette smoke when meeting his flock.

Every night it was the same. He told himself he'd have the one glass of Scotch Whiskey and always he had three. He'd prayed for the strength to resist the urge but had not prayed with any real conviction. He liked having three drinks. It was delicious, this Whiskey, *Laphoaig*. And even at the rate he was going through it there were always extra bottles in the cupboards below. Frank Power, the one-time Chief of Police, rarely came for his weekly visit without bringing a bottle as a gift. Frank did something in the backrooms of politics these days, the Archbishop wasn't sure what. Frank was a good Catholic, that was the main thing.

The Archbishop would watch the National News with his third drink and then go off to bed. He could hear the television now but could not remember what he'd been watching. Parishioners kept telling him he should get Netflix, but he had a phobia of technology and would stick with old-fashioned tely no matter how uninspiring the offerings.

He turned to go back to his comfortable perch in front of the television set and got such a start seeing Father Mackay standing in the room that he jumped and a quantity of the whiskey from the glass splashed out onto his hand and the arm of his sweater.

"The Devil! Mackay! Let yourself in, did you?"

Father Adam Mackay looked ghostly. There was finger's breadth of air between his collar and his neck. His eyes were rung with agitated red as though he'd been crying. His tweed jacket looked vaguely oily. His hair was surely thinner than when the Archbishop had seen him not a week ago. Ravages to be expected, supposed the Archbishop, in a man who was to surrender himself to police custody in the morning.

"Money can buy his silence. It is that simple," said Mackay.

"It's too late for that! He's already given a statement to the police."

"He'll recant. He'll refuse to testify," Mackay could not speak without losing his breath. "It's only ever been about blackmail with that boy. Was then, is now. He's an operator that one."

"Even if we cared to pay," said the Archbishop, "we are in no position to do so, we haven't the resources. How much money are you talking about?"

"I don't know. **I don't know!** I'll speak to the little whore's confederates. They'll name a price. It will be a great deal of money I'm sure."

"You are talking nonsense. Imagine if it got out that we paid for the boy's silence. Besides, we don't have a 'great deal' of anything but woes."

"We have plenty."

The Archbishop said nothing.

"There is an American in town. He's figured everything out. He knows that there is treasure here."

"It isn't 'treasure.'"

"This American is rich."

The Archbishop shook his head. "I suppose the boys taught you housebreaking. How did you get in here, Mackay?"

The Archbishop went to walk past Mackay, to investigate how the disgraced priest got in.

Mackay's arm swung and the whiskey glass was knocked from the Archbishop's grip. The Archbishop heard the crystal exploding against a wall and then felt a thunderous blow to the side of his head, to his temple.

He couldn't remember falling. He was on his front, face on the rug looking at the legs of the dining room table. Mackay's heel came down on his back. He felt his ribs crack, the wind leaving him.

"Where is it?" Mackay shrieked. "Where is it?!"

June 3, 2019

Inspector Vivien Ellis had only once attempted to give her presentation to elementary school kids out of uniform. Out of costume they didn't take her seriously and went rapidly from distraction to riot. In full regalia, wearing her side arm, the kids were rapt. Whether it was awe or fear, Vivien didn't know. If she had her own children maybe she would better be able to make sense of them.

Now near the end of her spiel she was getting too warm and needed to take off her cap. She was going to lay it on the teacher's desk, but Miss McAdams had her hand out ready to hold it.

"Let me," she said, smiling. Miss McAdams hadn't stopped smiling at Vivien since she arrived. McAdams was small, you might say mousey. Vivien was five foot eleven and supposed she had ten inches on the Grade 3 teacher.

"So," Vivien returned her focus to the students

in the classroom. "even if you know the person offering you the ride, even if it's someone from your street, a neighbour, you still need to check with a teacher or your parents to see if it's okay. Everybody get that?"

A boy near the front put up his hand.

"Yes?"

"If I gets into a car with a stranger..." the boy sniffed snot from his upper lip back up his nose, "do I still have to put on my seat belt?"

"Okay...good question, but I'm going to go back a little and explain some stuff again."

***

Walking her to the school's front door Miss McAdams still had Vivien's cap, was in fact, keeping it against her chest with crossed arms. Vivien carried a banker's box containing the props from her street proofing and car safety presentation.

"It must be difficult, on your partner, they must worry about you constantly when you are at work," said Miss McAdams.

"My husband is also a cop, so..."

"Oh," said Miss McAdams making little effort to hide her disappointment at the information for which she had been fishing.

"Soon to be ex-husband."

"Oh!" chirped Miss McAdams brightly.

"And I'm no longer in the field, not in the line of fire. I do this stuff mostly now. Community outreach." They had reached the front door of the school. "You can leave the kids in the classroom unattended like that?"

"For about thirty seconds. Give them five minutes and I'll have to call an ambulance; someone will have stabbed someone with a pencil, or someone will have swallowed a thumb tack."

Vivien reached out for her cap which the teacher reluctantly surrendered.

"If I told I was in possession of illegal narcotics," said Miss McAdams, "would you be obliged to search my person?"

Being mistaken for a lesbian was karmic justice, the cosmic settlement of score for Vivien pretending to be one in order to deflect the attention of a couple of guys, one of them quite married, who lived in the apartment building into which she had recently moved.

"Not going to happen," said Vivien.

"I had to try," said Miss McAdams. "I think it must be the uniform."

"No worries."

***

It wasn't unusual for there to be some media commotion in the lobby of the Police Headquarters

Building but Vivien had to make her way through a particularly large and animated crowd. There was a big crime story. She could not guess what and cared even less.

Through a grove of journalists, a couple of video cameras perched on their shoulders, camera phones held aloft she could see her soon to be ex-husband, Mark, talking into his cell phone. He had an arm straight out holding the reporter from the St. John's Telegram at a distance. So, the journalist could not overhear Mark's conversation she supposed. Mark looked exhausted.

Vivien swept her passcard over the scanner and entered the secure inner offices. Once inside she had to sweep her card again to unlock a turnstile, this gateway guarded by a large woman, a civilian employee, Eleanor something. As soon as Vivien's card passed Eleanor spoke to her via a speaker.

"Inspector Ellis."

Vivien walked to Big Girl's plexiglass cage. It occurred to Vivien that the speakers were superfluous, Eleanor could simply raise her voice to communicate with cops passing through the turnstiles. Now, even with them standing only two feet apart Vivien saw Eleanor was speaking into a microphone.

"Yes?"

"Inspector Ellis, you are to report to Superintendent Deveraux immediately."

"Okay. Thank you."

"It's urgent."

"They said that?"

"Yes, they did."

"Thanks."

Vivien couldn't see what police business involving her could possibly be 'urgent' so first went to her desk to deposit her bankers box and to check her email. Her mother, as usual, had sent three messages. One, a reminder they were to meet in her office at the university and two others that were just ramblings about politics, local and global, peppered with links on which Vivien rarely clicked. There was something from Vivien's lawyer, Joanne Dorsey, concerning the terms of her pending divorce that she would read later.

Superintendent Margaret Deveraux was only a few years older than Vivian. Deveraux was already racing up the chain of command when Vivien was a cadet. Deveraux's ambition was so naked, so unmasked that it didn't bother anyone, she was never faulted for it. She was steadily working her way up the ranks and was being groomed to be the force's first female Chief of Police before she was fifty years old. There was now rumour of a scandal involving the current Chief, corruption of some sort involving the Police Union so her promotion to the top rank might come any day. Deveraux was contender to someday be Commissioner of RCMP. She was also coveted as a potential candidate by every political organization in the Province and the Country. Devereaux's family were third generation military, her older brother was an already an Admiral in the Canadian Navy. She was born and bred to it.

Vivien's late father, Jack, had been an X-Ray Technician. Her mother, a university Classics Professor, said Jack was actually a very talented visual artist who couldn't make a go of it in the cultural backwater that was Canada. He gave up image making altogether when he faced the realization that it would be little more than a pastime. Vivian couldn't even recall him doodling. Everyone was surprised that Vivien went into policing, even, in a way, Vivien herself.

Vivien did not begrudge Devereaux her success. Her single resentment was that Devereaux wore clothes so much better than she did. She surely had half the free time Vivien did to shop and yet was always in something precisely tailored and suited to the occasion at which it was worn. Her business attire was conservative but always sharp.

Vivien could never find anything that flattered her (she thought herself too lanky, too flat-chested), so was jealous of all women who could, even though she knew that only meant they'd put in the hours hunting for clothes that she would not. Vivien was slightly uncomfortable and self-conscious in whatever she wore, a fact that made being in uniform a relief and gave her almost an extra hour of the day she would have spent fretting through three different outfits before giving up.

The superintendent rose from her chair as Vivien entered and bid Vivien sit down. Today, Vivien's superior was in an unusually sexy get-up: a matching boxy blazer and pencil skirt in tweedy woolen weave of charcoal, red and saffron. It was very near the line of what would be appropriate for a senior police officer at work. The garment took nearly a decade off Devereaux. Vivien wished she owned it.

Superintendent Deveraux sat. She took the string of tea bag dangling from a steaming mug and began lifting it gently up and done, as if she was fishing in the hot drink. She offered Vivien no refreshment.

"I am assigning you," Deveraux said, "to a case. Suspicious death. Body is in a car on the Cuckold's Cove Road, down by Quidi Vidi. Want you over there and beginning an investigation within twenty minutes."

Vivien felt as if she had been slapped.

"No."

"*No?*"

"I'm in community policing."

"Let's be clear, this is an order."

"Community policing is where I want to be. You're aware of my situation."

"What you want is irrelevant. I am aware of your situation and the force has been very accommodating. But you have not formally filed anything asking that…"

"Is this punishment for something?"

"Don't be ridiculous and be more mindful of our respective ranks in conversation. We are up against it. We have a lot of very serious matters at hand. I don't have a choice. You are the only officer I have available capable of taking this on. The dead man is an American citizen. It's hot, I cannot assign it to any of our resident morons. Just get down to the crime scene, pronto, and report. I don't have anyone else I can trust to get that much done right."

"Who says I'm capable?"

"Your husband, for one."

"Fuck that."

"I've heard otherwise," Devereux withdrew the

tea bag from her mug and threw it into a metal garbage pail making it ring like a bell. She appeared to want to stress that she knew what she'd said was cruel. Vivien was being insubordinate and had it coming. "You'll be working the file with Gerry Vatcher, he's waiting for you."

"Vatch?"

"Very possibly his final major case before retirement. Be nice for him to leave the force on a high note. Now go, they want to get the body out of there and open the road before it becomes an attraction. Hikers and dog walkers frequent the area."

***

Vatcher was waiting to be called on, he'd already received his orders. Vivien thought he looked like he was playing solitaire on his computer when she beckoned him to follow her.

She had the keys to an unmarked police vehicle. They were walking across the lot to the Impala they'd been assigned before Gerry said a word.

"Economy booms, crime goes up. It goes bust, crime goes up."

"We get it coming and going Ger, good for the law-and-order business."

They reached the car and Vivien opened the driver's side door.

"No, no, you drive," said Vatcher.

Vatcher closed the passenger side door behind him and adjusted the seat backward. Vivien still had not turned the key in the ignition.

"Are we waiting for something?" Vatcher asked.

"Your seatbelt."

"You're kidding."

"I am not, Ger. I've been going around to all the schools and telling all the kids that putting on their seat belt has to be a reflex, the first thing they do every time they get in a car until they do it without thinking."

"I have months left in this job, Ellis, my children are grown and have moved to the mainland. If I want to die in the crash, that's up to me."

"I'm not starting the car until your belt is on. Where you're a grown-up, especially."

"You think I'm a grown-up? I usually wait until the beeping makes me crazy."

Gerry Vatcher reached for the shoulder belt and, wheezing from the effort, put it on. Vivien turned on the car and they pulled away.

"How many accidents where the victim was ejected from the vehicle have you seen in your career, Gerry?"

"Enough that they have all merged into the one nightmare."

"How's that go?"

"A young man, his head on backwards, is up in a tree."

"You saw that?"

"Arrived at a scene. Car was a wreck. No victim. Took us ten minutes to locate the body, this girl, nineteen years old, in a tree. In the dream it's a young man, dunno why."

"Yeah."

***

A gravel road, so discreetly situated as to be unknown to most city residents, led to Cuckold's Cove, a picturesque little bay, with a lookout, overflown by ravens and bald eagles, at the very eastern edge of St. John's. The city ended here, at cliffs plunging into the Atlantic.

Passage down the road was blocked by a police cruiser. When the young Constable manning the post recognized Inspectors Ellis and Vatcher he waved them on, indicating how they should go around the front of his vehicle. His expression was grave, there was no colour in his face. Whatever was down there was gruesome.

Round the first bend, just where the vast, lead-coloured sea came into view out the driver's side window there was a further cluster of police cruisers, surrounding, at a distance, a dark blue sedan.

"3 series BMW." observed Vatcher.

Vivien stopped the car. She and Vatcher got out.

"You go on," said Vatcher, "I gotta take a piss."

The cops on the scene tried not to betray their surprise seeing Vivien walking toward the BMW. But if she was there it was clearly because she had been sent.

Vivien noted the car's careful finish.

She looked through the driver's side window. There was a dead man behind the wheel, his back arched slightly so his head was tilted back, his mouth hanging open. One gold tooth was visible. He was in his sixties she supposed. His trunk was badly burnt. Even with the windows closed she could detect the sickening scent of charred human flesh.

Another uniform came to stand a few feet behind her. Vivien turned around, it was Sergeant Neary, still a Sergeant.

"Inspector Ellis?" Neary made a face.

"Yes, Neary. Something wrong? Other than this man having been barbequed in his car?"

"Surprised to see you at a crime scene is all."

"Not as surprised as me."

"Back in the saddle?" he asked.

"I'm in community policing, this is temporary,"

"Okay. Got it." Neary consulted his notebook. "Car is a rental, from a private outfit, not one of the big agencies. It was delivered to the deceased at the airport. On a corporate card, Gustave Redding Leonoidas Polk. U.S. citizen. One of the boys said probably an oil guy but we don't know yet."

"Yeah, good guess, and I daresay Louisiana is the sort of place you find a 'Gustave Polk,' said Vivien.

"So, you are the investigating officer? Or... what?"

"Me and Ger, only until they can assign someone else. Do you have...?"

Neary was already holding out a pair of blue nitrile gloves for Vivien. Vatcher had caught up and was looking in the sooted window at the corpse. "Jaysus Murphy!" he observed.

Vivien opened the driver's side door with two fingers on the very edges of the handle. A stomach-churning gust of stink came from inside, burnt flesh and hair, meat gone bad and something higher, more volatile. Vatcher took a step back. Vivien heard Sergeant Neary gag.

Indeed, the man, the presumed Gustave Polk, appeared to have caught on fire somewhere just above his belt. There was a large hole in his body rung by the scorched remains of an exquisite suit. His internal organs, slick pink and yellow, were on display. His chin was blackened underneath, a five o'clock shadow of char. He was balding, the little hair on his head, above his ears was singed. His arms hung by his side. His right hand was resting on the front passenger seat and Vivien noted a garish ring with a large gemstone. She could smell the deceased's shit now too.

Vivien bent over so she could put her head in the car, being careful not to touch anything.

"He is wearing a bespoke suit," she said.

"A *what*?" asked Vatcher.

"A suit tailor-made for him. Well made. From very fine wool. He was a prosperous fellow. I'd love to have some clothes made for me sometime."

"Did something, like a cigarette lighter, explode in his pocket?" wondered Vatcher.

"That would be some Zippo. Besides, I don't smell gas. Maybe he was killed before the fire and this was an attempt to destroy evidence?"

"Nah, not the way he's…like…in the seat. It's like the fire came at him when he was alive. Came at him fast."

"I think you're right, Ger." One of the deceased's pants pockets had been consumed in the fire. Vivian checked the other. Nothing. His jacket was burnt away to the inside breast pocket revealing an American passport with only a top corner, on the opening side, touched by flame. Gingerly withdrawing the document, she felt there was a cell phone in the pocket as well. She opened the passport.

"Yeah, confirmation this is Gustave Redding Leonoidas Polk, born Luling, Louisiana, November 2nd, 1951. Got a bag there, Ger? No other signs of violence, not defensive marks on his arms or hands. It came at him fast. He didn't even have the time to try and put it out." Vivien stepped back and out of the car. A wasp and then another buzzed around Vivien's head, the scent of Polk's blood was attracting them. Vatcher had a clear plastic evidence bag ready. Vivien dropped the passport inside.

She saw the forensics team had arrived; three of them at the back of their cube van, putting on their white Tyvek overalls, taping the sleeves and ankles tight. She thought now she shouldn't have touched the passport. "Make sure those guys are thorough with fibres in the passenger seat, I have feeling some one of interest might have been sitting there. Any idea at which hotel Gustave Polk was staying?"

"He rented a house," said Neary.

"Just himself?" asked Vatcher.

"As far as we know. It was one of those executive places. Car rental agency gave us 24 Shea Place."

"Swish," said Vatcher. "People on the street had a racket with City Hall over them allowing a rental property there. Was in the news...five or six years ago?"

Vivien peeled off the gloves and started back to her vehicle. Neary and Vatcher jogged to catch up.

"Suicide?" asked Vatcher.

"No note. No vessel to convey whatever accelerant was used."

"Sure, yeah. Accelerant, like gasoline?"

"Yeah, Ger, like gasoline. How long has Gustave Redding Leonoidas Polk been in town?" Vivien asked Neary.

"Four days."

"Then...shit," said Vivien, "it's murder."

Vatcher didn't want to hear this.

"No...wait, how is it murder?"

"The deceased doesn't have car or house keys on his person." Vivien said.

"So?" said Vatcher.

"So, somebody has them. Let's get to that rental property, my guess is whoever did this has already been."

***

It was the hour of the day that the residents

of Shea Place had the help in. The vehicles in the driveways were not Mercs and Jags but the house-cleaners' and nannies' dented older model Escorts and Kias. There was a florist's delivery van at one sprawling house and a landscaping company's flat-bed at the next. Over the years the houses on the cul-de-sac kept expanding over their prestigious footprints so the places were now shoehorned to-gether.

The driveway of 24 Shea was empty, so Vivien pulled in. It was a carefully maintained house, two stories, stone faced, modern. A newer build in good taste. People here had the money to knock down perfectly livable older spots to put up something fresh and indulge their ideas for home design.

"I'll check around back," said Vatcher, "I gotta take a leak."

Vivien knew there would be no answer but rang and knocked several times to be sure. She could hear the gas mower running in a neighbouring house's backyard and smell its exhaust and freshly cut grass.

She stepped back and went to the stone wall of the landing. She didn't need to climb up on it as she thought she might, on her tiptoes she could look in the living room window and see enough to know the interior had been ransacked.

She went to fetch Vatcher but he was already on his way back.

"The place has had a going over," he said, "could see in through a window in the back."

"Same," said Vivien. "Should I call in for a warrant?"

"I dunno, I mean what is the imminent danger? Polk is dead."

"Maybe there's evidence that points to the killer?"

"And?"

"Foreign national…maybe an American killed him and could be fleeing the country?"

"Lotta conjecture. Don't even *really* know he was murdered."

Vivien thought about it. Vatcher made sense. But the absence of the keys told her Polk was killed. Goddamn Deveraux putting her in this position. Shag it, she was calling for a warrant, let the superintendent pay the price for putting Vivien straight in the middle of the shit.

"I'm calling in for a warrant. Can you find someone from the agency that rents the place to get down here with a key?"

Vatcher commenced rooting around in his pockets for his cell phone, shaking his head to indicate his disagreement with Vivien's course of action, or perhaps with just ever making a call or taking action when it could be avoided.

***

The owner of 24 Shea, a scowling middle aged fellow, balding, in a striking green tweed suit showed up with a master house key. He seemed intent on reading every word of the search warrant.

"Just open the goddamn door," said Vatcher.

***

Off a spacious and sky-lit foyer was a smartly decorated living area. An empty cardboard box of a size a person could carry under an arm had been discarded and lay where it fell. The cushions from the couch and a couple of chairs were on the floor next to it. On one arm of the couch a book lay open, face down. Vivien could see it was a bible. A trail of Styrofoam packing peanuts led to a dining room.

The landlord squinted at the scene. "He declined housekeeping even though we strongly encourage it. It's included in the price," he said.

"How long did he have the place rented?" asked Vivien.

"Open, but he paid for three weeks."

"Did he say what he was doing here?" asked Vatcher.

"Did he?" The landlord looked at his shoes and pondered "I assumed it was offshore oil. Did he tell me that? I can't recall."

The dining room was more heavily littered with packing materials, there was crumpled paper and bubble wrap on the floor. On the dark wooden dining table surrounded by eight chairs was a seemingly random selection of objects and boxes and padded envelopes of various size. There were two rolls of packing tape, one half used the other full. A hole big enough to put one's head through had been cut in the wall. The landlord whined on seeing it.

"Box cutters I daresay," said Vatcher.

"Meticulous, hey?" said Vivien. She picked up a brooch from the table, it featured an Octopus, its head fashioned from what looked to be a large pearl, four of its tentacles clutching blue gemstones. If it was a genuine pearl it would be the biggest one Vivien had ever held. She thought the jewel delightful. She handed it to Vatcher.

"You've worked a few B & E's in your time, Gerry. Value?"

"Dunno, looks pretty nice."

Vivien took an inventory of the other items on the table. A candlestick. An oil painting no bigger than the face of an Ipad. An ugly mantle clock.

There was a book in a garish yellow dustjacket, "Call for the Dead" by John le Carré. There was a wine glass, red crystals at the bottom betraying recent use.

Vivien picked up one of the padded envelopes by barely pinching the corner. It was like none she had ever seen. It was of much heavier construction and had a plastic zipper that closed the pouch and a flap over that. It recalled those canvas envelopes the banks used for currency. The envelope in her hand was pre-addressed: 17 Capet Avenue, New Orleans, LA 70115. There was no return address. Laying the envelope back down where she found it, she spied a long rectangular, flat jewel box, the sort one might use to keep a necklace but a little too large for that purpose. She opened it. Inside there were five custom-sized, circular indentations in heavy felt. For coins she thought.

"When can I clear this stuff out?" asked the landlord.

"Don't touch anything." Vatcher said reproach-fully. "You said you were good for three weeks."

"How did Polk die?" asked the landlord.

"No cause of death has been determined. And you are to speak of this to no one." Vatcher said to the landlord before turning to Vivien. "I'll go look upstairs."

Vivien went to the kitchen.

After some hesitation, as if calculating whom he least trusted, the landlord followed Vatcher upstairs.

Polk had camped in a tiny area, near the sink, in a kitchen large and well enough appointed for renters who wished to entertain. There was an open takeaway clamshell containing the remnants of Indian food on the counter, a used fork in the sink. Vivien opened the fridge. It contained a one-liter container of orange juice, nothing else.

She poked through the garbage beneath the sink. More takeout packaging, several waxed cardboard cups from Starbucks. There were two empty wine bottles. She registered the names on the labels, *Stags Leap* and *Freemark Abbey*.

***

Wu De had found a vantage point that enabled him to watch the house Polk had rented without being easily seen himself. He had to do no more than look out his car's driver side window. He knew by the direction of the sun and the street's leafy canopy that looking back at his car from the steps of 24 Shea Place would give no view of his vehicle's interior. With his naked eye he'd seen the police, one a tall, attractive woman in uniform, the other a fat old man in plain clothes, arrive. He needed his binoculars to better ascertain what they were up to now, that an agent, or possibly the property's owner, had let them inside. The woman in uniform had disappeared from view, probably looking around the back of the house, maybe the kitchen area. She would find nothing. The plain clothes officer was in an upstairs bedroom with a book in hand. Wu De didn't recall seeing a book and worried, only momentarily, whether he had missed something. He was satisfied that these small-town cops would never grasp what was happening.

It had grown cold. Godforsaken place was right on the North Atlantic Ocean and when the wind came off the water the temperature plummeted. Wu De started the car and turned on the car's heater. He stored the binoculars out of sight under the front passenger seat and drove away.

***

Superintendent Deveraux was again working a tea bag in a mug, compulsively moving it up and down by its string in the steaming water like she was going to hook something in there. She didn't offer Vivien or Vatcher, sitting across from her, anything to drink. In fairness there were more papers piled on her desk than when Vivien had been in the office just eight hours earlier. No, it was more than ten hours. Everyone in the room was having a long day.

"The body is at the Medical Examiners," reported Vivien, "they won't have anything for us for a day or two, longer for toxicology."

"And you don't think it was a robbery?" Devereaux asked.

"No, but maybe. There was a case at his residence, for collectible coins I think, that was empty but who's to say when, or if, it was ever full. There were a lot of other valuable items left untouched. There was a Garrard brooch worth thousands of dollars."

Vivien felt Vatcher's eyes on her. She turned to him.

"There was a maker's mark, I Googled it. Bet the books were rare or collectible too. There was an old John le Carré novel and a bible."

"Upstairs on his night table there was another bible and a book about the Voyage of St. Brendan the Navigator, like a serious book, academic, with small print and footnotes and such. Maybe he was religious, maybe some kind of amateur scholar," said Vatcher. He opened his notebook.

"Receipt in his wallet says he paid four hundred dollars for the Garrard brooch at an antique shop on the west end of Water Street," he said. "He paid $5.25 for the novel and one of the bibles at a used bookstore."

"What sport," said Vivien. "I daresay all the other stuff there was similarly procured. We'll find he was…a collector."

"Takes an eye," said Vatcher.

"High stakes Antiques Road Show, Officers?" asked Deveraux.

"The search of the house was methodical," said Vivien. "The person or persons going through the place were keeping a cool head, and we are speculating that these same people were only recently in the presence of a badly burnt body, may have even been responsible for the death, and they stay calm, intent on finding something. They are dusting for prints now and doing door-to-doors but this doesn't look like the kind of outfit to leave a trace."

"Was Polk even in town long enough to find this sort of trouble?" asked Deveraux.

"Not even a week," said Vatcher. "Maybe he brought trouble with him."

Devereaux issued a sigh of exasperation.

"The Father Mackay business is quickly going shitstorm on us," Deveraux said. "I don't have a single investigating officer who showed up for duty this morning who has gone home yet. I want us to wait on the Medical Examiner's report before we even think *foul play suspected*."

Now Vivien thought Deveraux was actually a little breathless, was not sighing but almost gasping for air. The superintendent was under considerable stress.

"This Polk guy, the victim, turns out he was a heavy hitter in the oil business," Devereaux picked up a sheet of paper from her desk and read from it, "a 'farm-in' specialist or something. Extremely high stakes I'm informed. And...well...that means, given economic realities, it's politically sensitive."

"That's how he fed his habit," said Vivien. Vatcher and Deveraux looked confused. "His collecting habit," Vivien clarified. "I'm guessing now the book on the table was rare. Bet that little painting was by someone with a name. He travels the world on oil business and collects things. He travelled with pre-addressed envelopes in which to ship the stuff back home."

"You remind me, New Orleans police called back," said Devereaux.

"Called who back?"

"You. I assumed," said Devereaux looking for yet another piece of paper on her desk. "Here it is. Contact is Detective Charles Lafayette, with his direct line, his cell." Deveraux handed the sheet to Vivien who had no choice but to accept it. "You are to talk to no one there but him. Thankfully, they are trying to keep it out of the New Orleans media until they've chased some leads. Anything else?"

Vatcher consulted his notes. "He was on something called Losec, it's for stomach troubles, and there was an out-of-date medication, Sonata, in his shaving kit, it's a knock-out pill typically prescribed for people taking long flights. Whether there were one or more people in that house or whether they got what they were looking for...not something we could determine from observation. They dusted for prints, but they won't find anything, these people knew what they were doing."

"Ger is right," said Vivien.

"Anything else?" asked Devereaux of her detectives.

"One man," said Vivien, "travelling alone, in town for a week, rents a furnished four bedroom for three weeks. He's eating takeout and drinking fancy wine."

"Meaning?"

"Meaning maybe the best hotel in town didn't provide the level of privacy he needed."

"Housekeeping was included in the price," said Vatcher, "but Polk declined it."

Devereaux looked to the ceiling. "Fuck," she said.

"Political sensitivities understood but someone should talk to his associates in the oil patch," said Vivien. "Has to."

Devereaux brought a hand to her face, touching her forehead, shielding her eyes so that it was impossible to see her reaction.

"Cell phone in his pocket wasn't badly damaged," said Vatcher. "We're in the process of getting a warrant for his phone records. On the off chance the phone isn't locked we might get more."

"You're going to tell me his wallet was full of cash," said Devereaux.

"Safe in the back pocket of his trousers. Three hundred and twenty Canadian dollars and five crisp American bills," said Vatcher, "Shiny Chase Manhattan Credit Card I've never seen before. For rich folk I'm guessing. Louisiana driver's license. No other cards. Wasn't a Costco member. No family photos."

"So not robbery, not a killer who would think to make it look like a robbery."

"Or one that doesn't care how it looks," said Vivien.

"If it wasn't robbery or a bad date you also have to consider family as suspects. Ask this..." Devereaux looked back at the note. "...Detective Lafayette, if he knows of any troubles with the relations back in New Orleans."

Neither Vivien nor Ger said anything.

"Family, am I right?" the superintendent asked again. "Inspector Vatcher said so himself, maybe Polk brought the trouble with him."

"Who will be handling the investigation, ma'am?" asked Vivien.

"I'm not sure I understand your question, Inspector Ellis."

"It's very likely homicide, Superintendent. It's murder. It's Major Crimes."

"Congratulations on your transfer to the Major Crimes Unit, Inspector Ellis. You'll be joining Inspector Vatcher there. Dismissed."

***

Vivien marched from Devereaux's office to the desk of her soon-to-be ex-husband, Inspector Mark Williams. Even haggard, stressed, in need of a shave and a fresh shirt, Mark was a handsome man. When they first met, Vivien was happy to have found a man tall enough, broad shouldered enough to take all of her in an embrace. He was athletic by nature, finding his bliss on the court or in the rink. He was good in the sack. He even cooked. He was a trophy catch she was releasing back into the river. Nobody could understand her decision. Everybody liked Mark. Vivien's mother loved him.

Mark could see Vivien's anger at a distance and braced for her assault by clutching the arms of his chair.

"Are you…I dunno? Trying to get back at me, or something? Trying to hurt me?" Vivien said.

"My superior," Mark was keeping calm, making himself speak clearly, "asked who was available and capable and you were top of that list."

"Fuck off, Mark."

"Okay, I'm flattering you. You were the only qualified person left to put on the list."

"Have I missed something?"

"Yeah, you have," said Mark who started picking overstuffed file folders from his desk, declaring the contents and then putting them aside. "Homicide from last week appears gang-related, killed by two dogs. Dogs! Another homicide last week, sex worker. No suspects. Another from two months ago, slam dunk, junior officer screwed-up the warrants so we are going to lose all the material evidence." He used two hands to lift a file thicker than a couple of city phonebooks. "A series of extremely ugly aggravated assaults related to the burgeoning trade in Chinese-made synthetic opiates. An otherwise professional arson for insurance that resulted in the death of a homeless person squatting on the premises. There's more. Wanna hear more?"

"Bad all over."

"Yep, bad all over and over again. You witnessed that clusterfuck in the lobby when our surrender failed to show and someone in this building decided they should tip off the media."

"This the priest?"

"Fadder MacKay, yep."

"He run?"

"No clue. Mackay's lawyer, Dennis Learning, he's is a good guy, always straight with me, and he seemed as surprised as anyone when his client didn't show."

"Serious charges?"

Mark picked Mackay's file from the others on his desk. "Full buffet; indecent assault — over 20 charges, invitation to sexual touching, buggery..."

"*Buggery*?"

"That's what the crime was called when the offences are alleged to have occurred so that's the charge."

"Victim was a minor."

"Name, *Freddie Dinn* ring a bell?"

"Does...somehow."

"Rent boy, drugs, stolen property and..."

"Yes, had a few weeks partying on a Cabinet Minister's credit card!"

"That's the lad. Your investigation, I recall."

"Maybe seven years ago?

"Nine. Freddie was an orphan and an altar boy."

"Two strikes. Are you suggesting Freddie is extorting Mackay?"

"Yes and No," said Mark, "I took Freddie's statements and I believe every word he said. But, you know, blackmail is in his DNA. Longer I'm at this everyone looks perfectly innocent and totally guilty at the same time."

"Maybe they are. There are situations where everybody is wrong. That's why I'm loving community policing, Mark, it's not law and order, it's public safety."

"Blowing this surrender makes us look stupid. Best case scenario we find Mackay's rotting corpse hanging from a beam."

"Why didn't you recommend Mercer take the body in the car? Gruesome death totally up his alley, more stuff for his scrapbook."

"Mercer's full time on the Stapleton fraud. Any further delays and that case is going to be tossed by the judge."

"Put Gerry Vatcher on the priest and you take the murder."

"Gerry's in the Knights of Columbus, one of his

uncles was a priest, another was a Christian Brother. He is waaaay too Catholic; he marches in a sash on Paddy's Day, with a sword," said Mark. "You determined the dead guy in the car was a murder?"

"Yeah, one hundred percent. Get Dooley to take it, he's marginally competent."

"On leave. Stress."

"Like us all," said Vivien.

Mark lost his patience. He almost yelled.

"You're ranked *Inspector*, Viv!"

To her relief Vivien's cell phone sounded, giving her an opportunity to avoid Mark's judgment. She read the text and turned on her heels. Mark called after her, loud enough that people down the hall could easily hear, "Community policing is hiding."

Vivien called back, to Mark and to the crowd, "That's the point."

***

Vivien's mother's office at the university was the only one Vivien could ever remember her occupying. Her mother, Louise, insisted she was once, when Vivien was a child, in an office yet smaller. Vivien doubted smaller offices existed and the tiny one her mother was assigned had shrunk steadily over the years as the walls grew thicker with bookcases, stacked boxes of files, saved copies of various academic journals, The New Yorker and The Times Literary Supplement, quantities of paper that only now, when she was emptying her office at retirement, it was clear there was no point in keeping in the first place. This was life, thought Vivien, the collection of things to be later discarded. The devaluation of accumulation.

Louise had always cultivated the look of an eccentric scholarly: dishevelled, a costume of clashing patterns, long scarves and high boots. But lately, as the years weighed down it was verging to negligence. There was what Vivien supposed was a stain from yesterday's lunch on her mother's dress and the silk around her neck was a few years late for an appointment with a dry cleaner.

"Should we have invited, Mark?" asked Louise.

"You're not serious?"

"I was very fond of Mark. And it's better to have your children when you're younger. It's too taxing to get down on the floor and pretend you're a dinosaur when you are in your thirties."

"Not having this conversation." But Vivien, as always, got drawn in by her mother. "In my *thirties*? Not giving me a whole lot of time."

"I'm not saying you should go back with Mark,

only that you could have gotten knocked up before leaving him. Or even now, just fake some make-up sex until you get pregnant."

"This is…I don't know what it is. Is it a selfish want of a grandchild on your part?"

"Yes, that's part of it. It might be most of it, but I lack the self-awareness to judge"

"Where is your send-off being held?"

"Faculty Club. Can no longer afford anything splashier; cut-backs, administrative bloat…I won't bore you repeating it all again."

"Please don't. I already know more about the crisis in the contemporary Academy than I ever will about policing." Vivien picked up an academic journal from her mother's desk. It was covered in dust with a sticky feel and twelve years old. "Are you going to get drunk and embarrass your daughter?"

"Oh yes, very much so. This may be one of my last chances to mortify you in a public setting." Louise took the journal from Vivien's hand, looked at it and sighed before shoving it into an overstuffed green garbage bag.

"At least you're opening up a position for some young scholar."

"In the Classics Department? No, nothing I taught has much retail value anymore. The position is attrition. They need more administrators. Come on, I'm thirsty."

***

The Faculty Club appeared to have been forgotten by the university administration sometime in the 1980s. Its condition supported Louise's contention that the education and research part, ("piece" in the latest parlance) of the university was now of the lowest priority, they were retailers of undergraduate degrees, fund raising machines and jobs for MBAs first. The Faculty and staff attending her mother's retirement were split down the middle between those who loved and those who loathed Professor Louise Harbauer, those who wanted to be there and those who were obliged to attend. About Vivien's mother no one was undecided.

Having quickly downed three glasses of white wine from a box provided by the university Louise was primed for conflict, so Vivien was keeping a close eye on her. Her mother considered argument a kind of sport and never accepted that for others it could be strife.

A young professor Vivien earlier caught studying her ass was now trying to impress her with smart talk. She could tell he mistook her for a fellow member of the Academy.

"Gerhard Richter," he said "in retrospect is THE

painter of the late 20th century. And I mean in a *painterly* sense. And that artist, whoever she or he was, was always going to emerge from Germany, nowhere else."

"I saw a show of his," said Vivien, "Big retrospective."

"Which one?"

"The Pompideau, in Paris. Knocked my socks off."

"I bet." The man extended his hand. "Professor Kyle West. Are you the new appointment in the Philosophy Department?"

"Vivien Ellis. And, no, Louise is my mother, I'm here to drag her home once she's had too much to drink."

"But you..."

"I'm not a scholar. I was in Paris on vacation with my ex. You know, desperate and ultimately futile attempt to save the relationship. Paris gets a lot of that traffic."

This sad account seemed to brighten Kyle.

"What do you do?" he asked.

"I'm a cop."

Kyle's expression betrayed disbelief. Vivien had seen the same face many times before.

"You know," Vivien expanded, "cracking heads, stealing drugs from dealers, taking bribes, planting evidence."

Across the room Vivien's mother cackled at something. Vivien turned her attention from Professor West.

"People thought that paper was a spoof, Henry," Louise was shouting," They thought you were trying to be funny! People were calling it 'The Terrington Hoax.'"

"I'm never without my handcuffs," Vivien said to the professor. The remark brought a flush to Kyle West's cheeks. First the schoolteacher, now the professor, perhaps educators were predisposed to harbour a fetish for cops. Probably craved punishment. "Tonight, it looks like I will be using them to restrain dear Mama. Won't be the first time."

June 4, 2019

The morgue was almost odorless. Almost. Vivien couldn't exactly smell death but there was something in the air, barely out of the range of perception, some part of decay that couldn't be scrubbed away or vented or masked that triggered a twinge of revulsion. Maybe it was all in her head. She'd met the Medical Examiner, Dr. Lionel Giroud, (everyone called him, unaccountably as he was from Quebec, "Scotty.") on several previous professional calls. Scotty was as sensitive to the squeamishness of those outside his grisly trade as she supposed anyone who spent their days with the dead could be.

The remains of Gustave Polk lay on a table between Vatcher and herself and Scotty. Stripped bare, bluish under deliberately telling lights, Polk looked even worse than he did in the car. The hole burnt in his body was larger than it had first appeared, and lower and more to the left of his trunk. His exposed organs no longer shone with moisture as they had when Vivien first saw them, they were now matte and desiccated. Scotty was using tweezers to pick a piece of something, half the size of a lentil, from the edge of the wound. He deposited it in a kidney shaped pan sitting high on Polk's chest, below his chin. Vivien knew that Scotty always took pains to preserve the dignity of the deceased and thought this oversight, using the corpse as a kind of shelf, was a function of him being unusually preoccupied with his task. Scotty held up the little particle for scrutiny, giving Vivien a welcome opportunity to raise her eyes from Polk.

"Retrieved several of these," he said. "Delivered, I suspect, via a puncture in his abdomen."

"I don't follow," said Ger.

"Nor I," said Vivien.

"I speculate this agent was introduced within the victim by injection, or, I suppose, punching a small vessel containing it through Mr. Polk's abdominal wall." Scotty brought his tweezers back to the metal pan and deposited the sample there. "And while that sounds unlikely, I cannot think of another explanation for these wounds."

"Like a tablet? In a capsule?" asked Vivien.

"There are small fragments of what I'm confident is glass in the vicinity, so yes a glass ampule."

"And this 'ampule' contained what?" asked Ger.

Scotty grinned.

"Took me a while to figure it out."

He paused for dramatic effect, but he quickly saw his audience wasn't up for a show.

"Alkali metal."

Vivien shrugged.

"Means nothing to me," said Ger.

"Sodium. Potassium," said Scotty. "Cesium?"

"Sodium, for me, is something I'm supposed to reduce in my diet," said Ger.

"Come," said Scotty. He lifted the metal dish from Polk's chest and escorted Vivien and Ger to a stainless-steel laboratory work bench.

He set a beaker, two thirds full of what looked like water, before them.

"These samples were all pulled from subcutaneous fat on the victim. That is why they didn't burn." Wielding his trusty tweezers again, Scotty picked up a piece of the mystery substance from the metal dish. "You will recall from your high school chemistry..."

Vatcher made a face that told both Vivien and the Medical Examiner that he failed high school chemistry. It made Vivien laugh perhaps because nerves made laughter a necessity under the circumstances. Scotty continued with his demonstration.

"...if you had paid closer attention you would recall that alkali metals are strongly reactive with water."

Scotty dropped his tiny sample into the beaker. There was a popping noise that gave Vivien a start, the little bead was skating around the surface of the water sizzling fiercely.

"Some party trick," said Vatcher.

"Unfortunately for Mr. Polk," said Scotty, "we are sixty percent water."

"Someone in the passenger seat stabbed Polk with something, some device..." Vivien was thinking aloud in order that the Chief Medical Officer or Vatcher could catch her in any errors in the conclusions she was drawing. "So, unless it was a hitchhiker packing alkali metals, the killer was known to the deceased and came to their rendezvous intending to, or at least prepared to, murder Gustave Polk."

"And," Vatcher joined Vivien in voicing his thoughts, "the victim is new in town so maybe he came here to meet the person that did the jabbing?"

"Yeah," said Vivien.

"It cannot have been," said Scotty, "a pleasant way to go."

***

Superintendent Devereaux had leafed back to the front page of the report and started again, twice, reading through each time quicker than the last. She shook her head in disbelief.

"No chance Polk swallow this alkaline stuff?" Deveraux asked.

"Alkali Metal. Alkaline could mean like...lye, like in soap," Vivien answered. "And no, Medical Examiner is fairly confident it was delivered via a perforation in the abdomen wall. He found pieces of glass that support that conclusion. I suppose though it is possible he ingested it orally. I should have asked. But I mean that would have been the first thing Scotty ruled out, no?"

"It was pretty fucking gross," said Vatcher. "Big hole burned in the guy."

Devereaux tossed the report across her desk toward where Vivien and Vatcher were seated, as if she was rejecting it. "What the hell is this?" she demanded.

"Obviously," said Vatcher, "First degree murder."

"You think?" Devereaux said with more sarcasm than became someone of her rank. She rose from her seat. "This is like...something to do with an intelligence agency or organized crime, right? Is it? Do I call the RCMP? Skip straight to CSIS? I trust his name didn't appear on some Interpol list? Are we sure the passport is authentic?"

"New Orleans police wouldn't haven't contacted us about an alias," said Vatcher.

"All we can say at this point," said Vivien, "is that the act appears to have been committed by a professional."

"A professional killer? That's a hundred percent?"

"Or a chemist."

"When was the last professional assassin in St. John's? Jesus, they probably used a sword, not an ampule of..."

"Alkali metal," said Vatcher.

"Thank you," said the superintendent.

"Most likely from out of town," said Vivian. "Someone who couldn't easily access the sort of weaponry they wanted here, just slipped in with his or her hidden device? So not bikers. But it appears to be a scheduled meeting, and one held deliberately out of sight. Victim and killer knew one another...or this was a first meeting, arranged in advance. The killer was allowed access to the car. It wasn't one of our usual suspects. It's too sophisticated for any of the local villains."

"*Sophisticated* is a word for it," said the superintendent.

"Perhaps it was to do with his business dealings, something in the oil patch," offered Vatcher. "There would be engineering types who would have the knowledge required to fashion some kind of 'fire knife.'"

Deveraux shook her head vigorously as if she did not want to consider the possibility.

"Or family. It could be family trouble that followed him here from New Orleans. A hit commissioned by someone down there? Victim doesn't know anybody here, he's more likely to let someone he knows in the vehicle. Do we know he travelled here alone?"

"We do. He was a single passenger to get off a private jet. That the trouble followed him from Louisiana fits with one story, but why here? Is it coincidental?" asked Vivien. Devereaux retrieved the report she had discarded and checked something.

"Alkali Metal?" Devereaux thought for a second and then commanded, "Pursue the family angle. Find out what this guy left behind in New Orleans. We clear the family, and you can run down the oil angle."

June 5, 2019

To get to New Orleans Vivien had to fly via Toronto and Chicago, so had been 12 hours travelling when she arrived at MSY from YYT. She napped fitfully on the first leg but had been awake and uncomfortable coming from Chicago. Standing at the luggage carousel at Louis Armstrong International she was tired and disoriented. Otherwise, she surely would have noticed the approach of the considerable six feet and some inches of African American man who was introducing himself with his badge.

"Inspector Ellis? Detective Charles Lafayette. Welcome to New Orleans."

He was a handsome man, the build of an athlete, a one-time football player perhaps? No, not that bulky, but still big. And his grooming and the restraint in his choice of suit didn't fit that bill. He had good taste but wasn't a clothes horse. His one concession to vanity was smart blue frames for his eyeglasses.

"Oh…wasn't expecting…"

"Perhaps you missed some communications in transit. Our office was in contact with yours. I'm here to be of any assistance."

"Okay."

"You'll have a driver at least."

"That will be a great help." An alarm sounded and the luggage carousel started moving. "It's mostly the victim's family I want to talk to."

"You have any indication they were in any way involved?" he asked.

"None."

"I was going to take you around the station, introduce you to a few people but the Polk family is…like a lot of New Orleans establishment…they have old friends inside the Police Department."

"So, we skip the pleasantries?"

"Probably prudent, and you'll be done sooner. You say you have no reason to believe the family was involved. Then why…?"

"I have no reason to exclude any of the family as suspects either, the murder is an utter mystery at this point. My superiors would like nothing better than this to have been a grisly family dispute so as not to do anything to tarnish the reputation of big oil."

"Can that reputation be any further diminished?"

"I know, hey," Vivien saw her bag emerge from behind the strip curtain. "I mostly want to meet the son, gauge his response, demeanour."

"You good at that?" Charles asked.

"I'm not too shabby," said Vivien. Her bag was now almost in reach but before she could bend to collect it Charles already had it in his hand.

"The one bag?" he asked.

"How did you know that was my bag?"

Charles Lafayette's head went back, and he laughed to the stars. It was the sort of large laugh that made Vivien smile.

"Your bag?"

"Yes," said Vivien, "how did you know that bag was mine?"

"Demeanour? Your response, a change in your breathing or your attention when it appeared?"

"You good at that?"

"Is it your bag?"

"It is."

"Then, 'not too shabby.'"

Now Vivien laughed. She was in a strange place on a difficult mission and this man was, mercifully, making it a little easier.

When they left the terminal building it was like stepping into a hot bath. Her clothes immediately gripped her tight, as if she was caught in a snare. It was June 5th and when she checked the New Orleans temperature before leaving it was a reasonable 15 degrees warmer than St. John's. She had not accounted for the swampy humidity.

***

Vatcher couldn't help but wonder how much more money Terry Jedore made than he did. Young guy in the oil patch, working offshore, probably an engineer. Cops made decent money but these kids in the offshore made a fortune. Fit, handsome and prosperous, Jedore had it made. Vatcher the boy was a mediocre student. Vatcher the man blamed his parents for never once giving him grief over the middling report cards. So long as young Gerry passed, was a "C" student, was enough as he was surely, he was going to follow in his father's footsteps and serve in the Royal Newfoundland Constabulary. Back then you didn't need a whole lot of algebra for that job. If his mother or father had pushed him, even a little, Gerry Vatcher thought he'd have accomplished more in life than having made it to retirement. He was capable of much more, especially back then, as a kid. *Back then*, everything was 'back then' for Vatcher these days.

Vatcher was meeting Jedore on the bridge of a ship. Vatcher had been in such places on police business many times over the years and they were typically greasy, redolent of diesel and bilge, grubby. But the con of this ship, a supply vessel servicing the offshore oil rigs, was as clean as a surgery. The days of brawling drunk seamen in their taverns near to the port, the days of the crane dropping a pallet of smokes to burst open on the dock for Longshoremen's share, the days of the Portuguese of the White Fleet playing a pick-up game of footie on the apron, the days of young lads cutting tongues from the fish being landed on the South Side were gone. The people working at sea learned their trade in schools and colleges now. Where once you got the job because you came from a seafaring tradition, you got it now because you had acquired the latest certification. Gerry Vatcher knew this was all supposed to be part of progress, but it was so much less interesting to him. It was safer, more profitable and ultimately, sterile.

Terry Jedore, doubtless of many such certifications, an alphabet soup after his name, was telling Vatcher about his meeting with the late Gustave Polk.

"It was a long shot, I was surprised Mr. Polk was interested," said Jedore.

"But he was, and very," said Vatcher.

"Actually, he didn't seem particularly focused on the terms of a deal that day, he paid little attention to the details."

"He flew here from New Orleans on his own plane to speak with you and Ms. Hounsel in person. That seems like serious interest to me."

"He didn't want to talk business."

"You had a few drinks. You must have talked about something."

"He had questions about town, its history, actually more the history of Newfoundland. Mary knows quite a lot, so she and he were talking about that. He was very interested in everything she had to say or was doing a terrific job of faking it. He wanted to know where to eat. Wanted to know who the best antique dealers in town are."

"And who are they?"

"I don't know. I don't know any antique dealers."

"Did Ms. Hounsell?"

"I don't think so. She sort of knew, thought she knew some from a few years back but wasn't sure they were still in operation. That's…maybe I'm not remembering it right."

"You said a couple of drinks. Did you mean two?"

Jedore thought about it.

"I think…maybe I had three pints. Mary had the one drink. I can't remember how many Mr. Polk had."

"Was he at all impaired? Did he look at all drunk?"

"Not in the least."

"Any other vices you think?"

Jedore was puzzled by the question. Vatcher pointed his chin toward the waterfront where could be seen two young men, standing waiting for something or someone. At least some things never changed. Jedore still didn't put it together. Vatcher illuminated him.

"Those are male prostitutes."

"I've heard that. That wasn't the sort of conversation we were having with Mr. Polk."

"Or girls, or gambling. Did he wonder where he might buy drugs? Anything to put him in with bad company?" Vatcher paused. "I have to ask these questions."

"I understand that. No, nothing."

***

It made Adam Mackay sick to his stomach to be in these grim alleys and lanes. He detested the night world, that louche quarter of any city that served its sinners. They were worse now in the day, when some faint daylight could make it to the bottom of the brickwork channels to illuminate the filth and corruption under foot. And they were so often in sight of the ships in port, once being the places for sailors to answer their basest desires in their short time ashore, to commit every depravity, serve any addiction, before returning to the waves in repentance. Now the venal from all over came to these places to satisfy their base desires. They were a sort of theme park for the depraved.

A man of the cloth, a man of God, Mackay knew he was supposed to be forgiving. But was God not also a judge, and a wrathful one? What of those who would never repent, who turned away from salvation time and time again? They deserved to be punished as he was being punished merely for having succumbed to temptation. His prayers for forgiveness were going unheard and yet he was expected to absolve the unrepentant. Why was God testing him so mercilessly?

The young man ahead of him, leaning against the wall, soiled and torn jeans, his head covered by his hoodie (Mackay was in the same costume to avoid detection) was one of them, one of the devil's own agents that had lured Mackay to ruin. Mackay had to be careful. These places were closely watched by the police and he was now a much-wanted man, possibly 'most wanted.'

"What do you like?" the young man asked. Mackay was filled with revulsion, not at the question, but how, against all prayer and petition, it secretly thrilled him.

"I need to find Freddie Dinn."

"I does anything Freddie does." The young man had the sort of pronounced rural Newfoundland accent that Mackay most detested. Fifteen years since he had left his home in New Brunswick for this awful place and still the local dialects were discordant to his ear.

"I have to talk to Freddie. It's in Freddie's interest. Where is he?"

"Tell you what I knows for twenty bucks."

Mackay checked again to see that they were unobserved. He resolved that he would kill himself before being taken into police custody. There were too many boys for whom he had cared now in the prison system, too many set on revenge. But he would be bound and so prevented from taking his own life if suddenly apprehended on the street. He could not be too careful. Convinced they were unseen Mackay got out his wallet and handed the hustler a twenty-dollar bill.

"Sometimes he bees down to the El Tico"

Mackay needed more. "And?"

"Das it, dats all I knows."

Mackay grabbed the young man by the collar

and slammed him against the wall.

"Fucking tease. You're all teases!" Mackay could feel the man was quaking with fear, a frequently beaten dog.

"Dats all I knows, dats more dan most."

Disgusted, Mackay let him go.

"You're all alike."

***

Vatcher made his way back to his vehicle, passing as he went, the hustlers he had pointed out to Jedore. All his years as a cop taught him that despite the laws on the books, humans were going to do what their hearts and guts and genitals or voices in their heads told them. Thirty-two years of service and he knew how the world worked but knew always less why. A knowledge of life's harsh realities, nagging doubts about whether humanity could ever really be civilized, and a rotten prostate was what he would leave the police force with. The gland was tormenting him again now, telling him he needed to piss. Whether he did or not he would only discover having unzipped and stood waiting at a urinal or over a toilet. Sometimes after a moment of strain he issued a stream, more times it was a painful trickle. He was nostalgic for the days he pissed a torrent. How fucking sad was that, fondly recalling the days when he could take a slash without reviewing it. He was awaiting the results of a biopsy but simply assumed, feeling as unwell as he did, that the news would not be good.

A man stood past; his head covered by a hood. This made cop Vatcher instinctively seek a face. Man wasn't a known villain, too old to be a hustler, he had grey stubble on his chin so perhaps another sad john. Something else though. He hadn't gotten a good look at the shaded eyes. The man left a trail of body odor.

Fishing his keys out of his pocket Vatcher felt his need to urinate grow more urgent. Getting behind the wheel he sensed he wouldn't be able to wait until he got back to the station, he needed to go now.

Mackay! It hit him, that face! It was Mackay!

He looked out the rear window and already the figure was out of sight, likely having ducked down an alley. This was the way to end his career thought Vatcher, bringing in a most wanted man, taking him through the back door of the cop shop in cuffs, booking him. That was the way to be remembered, to leave his mark on the force.

He turned on the ignition and put the car into a u-turn in order to pursue Mackay. He had swung it around, put it in the other lane when he felt damp in the seat of his pants. He pulled over, shifted in to Park and began to weep.

New Orleans

Without Detective Lafayette as her wheel man Vivien would have likely been late for her first appointment as the Polk home was not an easy one to find. The grounds, once planned and attended, had been neglected for some years and now overgrown to the degree that thick ungroomed vegetation screened the grand house from the street. It was much the sort of building Vivien expected to see in New Orleans, an antebellum mansion, pillars and a wide gallery on the exterior.

All the first story's interior was, like the library in which Vivien and Detective Lafayette now sat, of dark woods, mahogany or walnut, that seemed to consume light despite every inch being polished and buffed to a high shine. The big rooms were furnished with pieces large enough to make them feel claustrophobic. The desks and cabinets and credenzas were all exquisitely made but mostly ugly things. Vivien didn't know enough to date them, but they clearly came from different periods, the only connecting theme being their grandeur and, she supposed, their worth. No room through which she had passed felt lived in, air did not circulate in this house. They might as well be in a mausoleum.

She and Detective Lafayette were pitched on an uncomfortable divan opposite a commodious high-backed leather chair that looked as if it might consume its inhabitant, Henri Polk. Vivien rarely heard and supposed she had never once used the term *fop*, but it came immediately to mind when she laid eyes on Gustave's son. Henri Polk was thin and pale skinned. He compulsively wet his lips. His hair, thick and slick with some product, was brushed back over his head with his hands. He appeared not to have showered that morning. He might have slept in the clothes he was wearing, matching jacket and pants of an ivory-coloured fabric with a fine pink stripe. He had on a robin's egg blue shirt, open one button too many at the neck. He wore cherry red leather loafers, no socks. Vivien found Henri Polk repellent but coveted the smart shoes.

"The body is still with the Medical Examiner in St. John's, the Coroner," Vivien explained. "It will be released as soon as possible, and your family can make arrangements for it to be returned to Louisiana."

"At your leisure," said Henri, "his death hasn't yet made the papers here. I'm not even sure there will be a funeral."

"Oh, I only thought, as your father was a pious man."

"Pious! My father? No, no, no."

"Not a practicing Catholic?"

"God, no," Henri laughed.

"My mistake," Vivien said, "we found two bibles at the house where he was staying in St. John's."

"Sure they weren't Gutenbergs?" said Henri.

"This is an unpleasant area of inquiry so if you don't want to answer I get it,"

"All ears."

"Do you know of anyone who might have wanted to harm your father?"

"Certainly, I've long wanted him dead. But I don't have the resources to hire an ass…assass…" Henri's speech impediment made its first appearance, "assasas…hit man. I'm sure there must be dozens of business associates with scores to settle, indeed some for whom his killing could be a business decision. I am not suggesting oil people are particularly villainous, only when such sums are involved…" Henri's voice trailed off. He looked as if he might nod off and then roused himself. "My sister often talked about doing it herself, slaying him. But not to worry, she is barely a viable human being. The degree of organization required to extinguish father is quite beyond her."

Henri's attention was momentarily diverted. Something was clearly making him physically uncomfortable. He fished around behind his back and withdrew a plastic pill bottle. He squinted at the label and then slipped the container into a jacket pocket.

"I doubt my sister," he continued. "Could even find Norway on a map." Henri laughed loudly at his own joke.

"Newfoundland," said Vivien. "Your father was murdered in Newfoundland. In Canada."

"So he was," said Henri.

***

Leaving the Polk mansion Vivien reflexively put a hand over her eyes to shield them from the sunlight. The interior of the place seemed even more deprived of illumination stepping from it. Charles led the way down a walkway, green growth seeming to ooze between the flagstones. He held a tall iron gate open for Vivien and closed it behind them. Walking down the drive, Charles asked, "So, demeanour?"

"Difficult to read through the veil of booze and pills. I wouldn't strictly rule out involvement, but he didn't have an air of guilt about him," said Vivien.

"Some people commit crimes for which they feel no guilt."

"True. But I doubt he could stay sober long enough to pull it off."

"I agree," said Charles. They reached the curb where several green garbage bags awaited collection. Charles reached down and picked up two of three of them. "Could you please you grab that one?" he asked. Vivien hesitated.

"Need a warrant for that in Louisiana?" she asked.

"Not according to California verses Greenwood in which the United States Supreme Court overturned the California Superior Court decision that held that the fourth amendment prohibited the search and seizure of garbage left *outside the curtilage of a home*."

Vivien picked up the other bag of garbage. "Not up on my U.S. law, I'll have to trust you."

"Fourth amendment is all the law surrounding warrants, probable cause. It's the amendment cops need to know."

Charles popped the trunk of his car. He put the

bags inside. Vivien did likewise. Charles looked up and down the street to see if they were being watched thought Vivien. "That overgrown yard keeps people from looking in, but it also keeps the people inside from looking out," he said.

"What do you think you might find in those bags, Detective Lafayette?"

"Henri might not have had anything to do with his Daddy's death but he ain't telling us all he knows." Charles paused. "Demeanour."

***

After he had wiped down the driver's seat of the police car he was assigned and changed his pants in the locker room, Vatcher went straight away to report his sighting of Mackay to Mark Williams. Mark was sympathetic, a fact for which Vatcher was grateful.

"I totally get it Ger, no worries, you couldn't pursue, it's still a good lead." Mark said. Vatcher couldn't understand why his new partner, Vivien, would have left Mark, he was a great guy.

"I was going to travel when I retired you know," said Vatcher. "Don't wait, Mark, do that shit now."

"You'll work it out. You're seeing a doctor?"

Vatcher nodded that he was.

"Gotta ask again, how confident are you that it

was Mackay?"

"Not very, but…I've been at this so long, Mark, you know, spidey senses."

"Get that. Was he like *cruising*, looking to pick someone up?"

"No, definitely not, his head was down, and he was in a hurry."

"Okay."

"Mark, I really wish I was bringing him to you in 'cuffs."

"Don't worry about it, Ger. We'll get this guy. Where's he gonna hide? It's enough to know he is still in town. Twenty hours…he will be in custody."

***

Charles had driven a considerable distance from the Polk mansion, crossed a long bridge over the Mississippi, to find a dumpster behind a boarded-up one-story industrial building. He gave Vivien a pair of blue nitrile gloves and donned a pair himself. As he and Vivien picked through the garbage, they examined each item and then tossed it into the rusting green bin.

"The cleaner was there recently enough to have put the garbage to the curb. This smells like a day in the sun, if that. Not more." Charles held up an empty wine bottle.

"1945 *Chateau Latour*," he read the label before tossing it into the dumpster. The glass smashed inside. Charles picked up another bottle, "*Domaine de Romanee Conti. 1966*. Know anything about wine?"

"Only the six bottles under twenty-five bucks that I like to drink. But 1945 and 1966, they are clearly collectors' items."

"Hundred percent," said Charles. "Betcha a case of your favourite plonk these are the sort of bottles that get collected and never uncorked. Seeing them there at his father's house, unopened, must have driven a lush like Henri to distraction. He's been plundering the cellar since he got the news that his daddy was meeting his maker."

Vivien examined several pieces of paper, fouled with household waste. "These are financial papers, simple bank statement, something regarding the commercial mortgage of a shipyard in Galveston, Texas. Doesn't give much away. I'm sure anything interesting goes to the office."

"But Henri was looking."

Charles picked up a rectangular case, very much like the one for holding coins that Vivien had seen on the dining table at the property Polk had rented in St. John's. "Pop it open," she said. "For coins."

Charles opened the case and indeed there were four custom sized depressions for holding coins.

"Saw some of those at the victim's residence in Newfoundland," Vivien told him.

Charles turned the box over in his hands.

"Mean something to you?" she asked.

"No, why?" said Detective Lafayette.

"Your breathing. Demeanour."

Charles laughed.

"So far as we know right now, Polk died intestate, no will. I venture the son and the sister cashed-in what they could right away. Tide them over until the estate is settled. And that'll be years."

"I had the same thought."

"I have an idea where Henri would have moved the coins."

There was a gunshot at a distance, Vivien judged six or seven city blocks. In a few seconds another.

"This parish is called Algiers. Gun violence is a terrible problem," Charles paused. "Jazz came from here."

"Jazz music?"

"That's right, from the musicians who played dance music on the riverboats, they started putting variation, improvised lines into the repetitive tunes the crowd called for them to play over and over again, up and down the Mississippi. Those cornet and clarinet and banjo players? Most of them lived here." Charles said. "America's music,

America's art form. And now everybody is shooting everybody else...there is something gnawing at the soul of this country. One day I think I get why, the next I'm at a loss." He gathered up the last garbage bag, almost half full, carried it to the dumpster and threw it in. He peeled off his gloves and tossed them in. "We've got to go back over the river."

***

Charles took them to what Vivien thought was called The Garden District. It was a leafy quarter, far more prosperous than Algiers, with the sort of buildings she expected to see in New Orleans. The antique shop stood out from its neighbours in being uninviting. The display windows exhibited little, a couple of ancient clocks, a sword in an ornamental scabbard — something from the civil war she supposed, an old table-top model of the solar system with the planets turned round the sun by means of a hand crank. There was no sign other than a small metal plate above the door, *Antiquaire St. Cyr*. The door itself was narrower than any Vivien had seen on the exterior of a building, Charles had to bend and turn somewhat sideways to enter.

Vivien knew little about antiques but the articles for sale in this shop seemed, to her untrained eye, of a particularly high standard. The window display was a ruse to keep away the merely curious. She thought about the delightful octopus brooch she found at Polk's rental in St. John's, it was the kind of thing she might see beneath the glass in an establishment such as this. Similarly, the proprietor here was better dressed than any antique dealer she had ever seen, but then, she thought those folks, back in St. John's, were running what were better described as junk shops. The gentleman at the counter was in handmade clothes such as the late Gustave Polk was found. Charles handed the dealer the empty coin case.

"Numismatics is not my province," the dealer said.

Charles flashed his badge. It was a formality, the dealer showed he knew they were cops from the moment they crossed the threshold of his business.

"But you knew enough to buy the coins in this case from Henri Polk?" said Charles.

The dealer paused to think. Not about the question, thought Vivien, but whether he should be calling a lawyer.

"Those examples would have been familiar to anyone with even a passing knowledge of collectible coins."

"What were they worth?" asked Charles.

The dealer clearly did not want to answer. His eyes met Vivien's.

"I gave Henri Polk one hundred thousand dollars for the four early American coins."

"That wasn't his question," said Vivien

"I operate a business, not a charity. He was welcome to take them elsewhere. I paid one hundred thousand dollars cash. Cash! I asked no questions. Discretion comes at a premium. It took some doing for me to put my hands on that sort of money so quickly. The banks won't do it."

"How much were the coins worth?" Charles asked again.

"There were only two in the case of great value. I saw those right away. The 1838 half eagle...which is likely worth about a hundred thousand dollars itself. I have to protect my interests; this is a business." The dealer adjusted his shirt cuffs and drew a breath. "And I have already resold the 1795 five-dollar piece for one hundred and seventy thousand dollars. Would have fetched more if I was willing to wait." Just as Vivien noticed the perspiration blooming on the dealer's forehead, he was mopping it with a handkerchief. Was it the Louisiana climate? "But," he continued. "I did not see any Roman coins. Henri didn't even know what I was talking about."

"What are you talking about?" asked Vivien.

"Henri's father, Gustave Polk called me…from the Canadian Arctic if you can believe it and asked about the value of some Roman era coins."

"Can you be more specific?" asked Charles.

"As I've said it isn't my area, in fact I don't understand why Gustave would ask me and not consult someone with greater expertise. They were silver Roman era coins."

"They must be valuable," said Vivien.

"Not necessarily," said the dealer," Many are quite common." He was getting agitated. "I should really have consulted with my attorney before speaking with you."

"Why? You're not under investigation unless your revelations about cash transactions suggest some tax avoidance." Charles said. His tone was friendly, he was smiling. "Daresay a lot of your business is strictly cash."

"This isn't a pawn shop. I'm always cooperative with the police. And receipts were issued, the income will be recorded. The transaction was completely legitimate. I'm not responsible for what Henri Polk does with his money or whether he pays his taxes. I'm by the book." He paused before repeating himself. "I am always cooperative with the police. You know that."

"I do know that, so I also know that you will keep this conversation between we three. Don't want the fox flushed out before we have our dogs in the hunt."

"As you wish."

"Thank you for your time," said Vivien.

"Yes," echoed Charles, "Thank you very much."

The dealer said nothing to acknowledge the thanks, ignored it, dipping his head to turn his attention to some papers on the counter in front of him.

***

Sergeant Kavanagh loathed these people, peddling their mouths and assholes in these disgusting piss-stained, rat-infested alleys. People could now buy whatever perversion they wanted from their smartphone and have it delivered to their hotel room but that wasn't what those who traded here wanted, they wanted the filthy, dank spaces behind the buildings, the parking garages, the city parks. That was central to the thrill of it. The one he had against the wall was a drug addict too. They were all fucking addicts. No surprise then when Kavanagh found a tiny wrap, the corner of a plastic bag tied off, containing some sort of white powder, in the cocksucker's jacket pocket. Who knew what that shit was, sold as cocaine but mostly speed, bit of ketamine and Oxy for bad luck. Kavanagh made a mental note to wash his hands thoroughly when he got back to the station. He should have worn gloves. Some of his fellow street soldiers had died from exposure to the latest scourge, carfentanyl

"Tell me now or I will bust your ass so hard you won't sell it for a nickel."

"I don't know!"

"Philly already told me you were talking to Mackay, that Mackay gave you money, so fucking tell me."

"Philly don't know. I wasn't."

"What did Mackay want?" Kavanagh demanded. "Was it just a trick you were turning, or did he want something else?"

"I wasn't. I wasn't."

Kavanagh swung and his fist hit the hustler square on the nose. He heard something break, not bone, something softer, some cartilage perhaps, and saw the blood and snot exploding from the blow. Again, he reminded himself to wash his hands. The hustler put his hands to his face.

"What did Mackay want?"

"Looking for Freddie Dinn."

"Okay, and where is Freddie?"

"I told Mackey, the El Tico."

"What the fuck does that mean? Any skeet could be at the El Tico any day of the week any hour of the day."

"I don't know."

Kavanagh hit him again, this time busting the prostitute's lip open. There was no fight left in the little shit. He was sobbing, blubbering.

"I don't know. I would tell you if I knew."

***

Charles Lafayette had taken Vivien to a bar far from the throngs of tourists who were, she saw, overrunning New Orleans. The exterior didn't look much different than the homes on the same stretch of road, two story wooden places, with verandas downstairs and balconies up. The red and green neon sign for the place, "La Petite Amie," was small enough you might miss it altogether if you weren't looking. Perhaps that was the intention.

The floor was in want of a mop but the bar where they were seated was wiped clean and the shrimp dish Vivien was polishing off was terrific. Charles demanded she take a bite of his sandwich, a Po-Boy with fried oysters and it was as good. The beer was served very cold.

A four-piece band was setting up. A ghoulish girl slinging a bass guitar over her shoulder was the only other white person in the joint. The frontman, a skinny, elderly black man, his hair a shock of silvery gray, in enormous sunglasses (Vivien took them to be women's) and faux snakeskin pants, was sorting himself in a chair in order to accommodate, in his lap, an accordion nearly as big as he was.

"Delicious. Really good. And we are particular about our seafood in Newfoundland. Sure beats airplane food. Excellent idea, Detective Lafayette. Full marks."

"I'm 'Charles' off duty."

"Never a Charlie?"

"Never."

"Not even to your mom?"

"Especially not to my mom."

"This place one of your regular haunts?"

Charles laughed. "My first time here. I read about it on a food blog."

"See, proof everything on the internet is true."

"Wanted to find a place we were unlikely to see any cops or cons I know."

"The New Orleans force that corrupt?"

"It's not the worst, but there is so much money at stake in the Polk estate, it would chum the waters. And where I am in the company of an attractive woman, there'd be questions. You know what it's like at a police station when there is nothing going down. Talk."

"Should have sent my partner Vatcher, nobody would ever want to know."

Charles laughed.

"My boss doesn't want any ripples in the oil patch, that's all she cares about." Vivien said. "We fucked our fisheries and offshore oil is all that keeping the place open."

"Same," said Charles.

Vivien finished her bottle of beer.

"Another?" Charles asked.

"I'll get in my seat on the plane, they'll put on the seatbelt sign, and I'll have to pee."

"Sure?" asked Charles.

Vivien checked her watch. There was almost four hours until her flight. "What the hell, you're driving."

The band announced itself with the hum of its aged amplifiers, the heavy electric thump of a jack being plugged in and the inhalation of air into the big squeeze box. They launched into a bouncing march and shuffle, the accordion playing a simple and joyous melody married to the propulsion of the bass and drums. "Hey ey yah," the accordion player sang and then some lines in something that sounded French to Vivien's ear, "Et toi!" It was irresistible. Even staid Charles could not but move to the beat. Those sitting in the bar had obviously been waiting for the music to begin for they were straight to their feet. The music pushed the hips side to side and bent the knees. Vivien wanted to dance so was pleased when Charles extended a hand. "One dance," he said. "And then I'll take you to the airport."

***

The only light cast over the interior of the El Tico Lounge came from three video lottery machines, a lamp over the cash register and a string of Christmas lights no one had bothered to take down. It wasn't that it was always Christmas but that at some Christmas, some years ago, Christmas ceased to mean anything here.

It took Adam Mackay's eye a few moments to adjust and make out the two men sitting at the bar drinking what looked to be short rum and cokes. There was a morbidly obese barmaid attending them. The only other life in the place, if life was the word for it, was a shrivelled crone blowing her pension in one of the fruit machines. The two men at the bar were not only openly smoking cigarettes but as Mackay approached, he saw one inhale a line of white powder straight off the bar. By whatever arrangement with whatever corrupt officials there seemed little worry at the El Tico that there would be a visit by any inspector. More likely they didn't dare.

"A beer, please, Jockey Club," Mackay said putting a ten-dollar bill on the bar.

The barmaid gave no indication she intended to serve him. She turned to the two men already parked at the bar, "Glen?" She was asking for instruction.

Glen lifted his head slightly, giving the okay to serve the intruder.

Both men were glowering at Mackay.

"I seen you," Glen said.

The barmaid took Mackay's money and gave him a beer, a Black Horse and not the Jockey Club he's requested. She provided no change.

"On television," said the other of the two men. They were bulky fellows, their prison exercise regime temporarily on hold their muscle was turning to fat. Mackay's interrogator had a poorly executed neck tattoo that, in the dim light, look like nothing but a blotch on his skin.

"You a movie star?"

"No, b'y, he's on the news."

"Bad news."

Mackay looked at them, they knew who he was, had found him guilty before hearing his side of things, knew he was wanted by the authorities but would never call the police on anyone, for anything, ever. "I would like to speak with Freddie Dinn," Mackay said. "I'm sure you gentlemen know Freddie."

Glen got off his bar stool and stepped toward Mackay, coming inside the range Mackay was comfortable with, close enough to smell, even taste Glen's sour breath. "I daresay Freddie is done talking with the likes of you, Padre."

The other man now stood. "What do you want Freddie for?"

"I know what he is looking for," said Mackay

"Do you?" asked Glen.

"I know that he will want to hear what I have to offer him."

Mackay never saw the first fist that struck his face. He put a hand up to fend off another blow and one of his two assailants bit it hard enough that he felt a bone crack. A knee to his groin put him on the floor. He was kicked in the head. He felt a tooth sliding on his tongue. And another. His left eye was rabidly swelling shut. He could taste his own blood, "I can pay him," he said.

"You don't *have the coin,* Fadder."

Mackay actually laughed.

"You tell Freddie," he said, "that I really do have the coin."

June 6, 2019

Vivien was sitting at Vatcher's desk trying to concentrate on what he had to report but her mind kept returning to New Orleans. On the plane ride home, she had thought of little else but Charles Lafayette. She was embarrassed that she had a little crush on her American colleague. But why not, he was a charming man, smart, good looking and tall enough for a tall girl like herself. He was a terrible dancer who didn't let it stop him from dancing. Any woman would have the same feelings about him as she did. It was the first time a man had been much in her mind since she left Mark. She didn't see a ring but felt uneasy about not asking whether he had a partner. One hundred percent, the guy was straight. Maybe it was a good thing. Maybe it was time.

She'd come straight from the airport to the police station to meet with Vatcher, who had copies of Gustave Polk's cell phone records laid out on his desk. She was running on far too little sleep.

"These were the calls out stored in the phone, I only went back three weeks," Vatcher said. "Twelve calls to coin dealers in London and Paris."

Vivien nodded. It was confirmed then, rare coins were the booty.

"Three more calls to outfits calling themselves 'Antiquarians.' A call to someone at the auction house, Christies, in New York. Business calls I suspect, local numbers in the oil play, Galveston, Houston, call to an offshore rig. Twenty-seven calls to residential numbers here in St. John's, nineteen of those to…get this…an Adam R. Mackay."

Vivien didn't get it. "Father Mackay? The Father Mackay there is an arrest warrant for?"

"What the fuck, hey?"

"Yeah, like really *what-the-fuck* what the fuck. Any idea what that is about?"

"None."

"Mackay is still at large, right?"

Vatcher checked his computer screen.

"As of a few hours ago, yeah. "

"Okay, we have to talk to Mark about this, see if he knows anything about it."

"Sure," Vatcher drew a breath. "You know Viv, I have, you know, a medical issue and it means I can't really be too far from a men's room. If, going forward with the investigation, I can ride the desk, do what has to be done here?"

"Absolutely, Ger, I completely understand."

"Thank you."

"So, you don't wanna come with me now?"

"Where?"

"To see Mark."

"I'm sure he's gone home by now."

Vivien checked her watch, she'd overnighted at an airport hotel in Toronto, taken a midday flight to St. John's and so lost the day.

"You're right. Fuck it, I'll go over to his place."

Vatcher shifted in his seat.

"You should call first."

"Something I don't know, Ger?"

"No."

"I left Mark, remember, not the other way around. I'm not going to be shocked if he's there with a new girlfriend."

"Can I be candid, Viv?"

"Yes."

"In my many years in policing I've been called to a great many domestic disturbances where the man or the woman who ended up in trouble had convinced themselves of that very thing."

"Thanks for the tip. I'll put my sidearm in the

locker before going over there." Vivien stood to leave. She had one more thing to say, "It's my house too, by the way. Until Mark buys me out, it's my house too."

***

Vivien rang the doorbell of the matrimonial home. After a moment Mark opened the door.

"You have a key," he said. "You could have let yourself in."

"Didn't want to surprise you."

"Gerry Vatcher called and told me you were coming."

They went to the kitchen. Vivien couldn't help but survey the place as she went, chart the changes since she had, of her own accord, left. The house did not look lived in. Surely, she imagined a layer of dust. Was there a stillness in the air, a quiet? Something one imagined. There was unopened mail on a table in the hall. A bag of hockey equipment, still full of its fetid cargo, had only made it as far as the door of the laundry room. From all appearances, Mark spent little time moping around feeling sorry for himself. It looked like he'd been too busy to miss her.

Mark got Vivien and himself a beer from the fridge. Vivien handed him the printout of Gustave Polk's cell phone traffic. It took Mark no time to spot Mackay's number.

"No clue. I have no idea why Mackay should have been talking to Polk. No idea. I am ashamed to admit we didn't spot this. This was Derek Holden's responsibility."

"Trying to make me feel like a shit for getting Holden in trouble?"

"No, in fact, I'll be the one taking the blame."

"Mackay's current whereabouts?"

"As you know, Gerry Vatcher thinks he spotted him downtown. We have some extremely unreliable sources that confirm he was down there looking for Freddie Dinn, presumably trying to convince him to drop the charges."

Vivien noted two cleaned wine glasses in the dishrack by the sink and teapot on the counter. Mark was a coffee drinker.

"It seems hard to accept that…" Vivien started, but Mark cut her off.

"I know how it seems, but don't you think with the public attention on this we don't have every resource tracking Mackay down? This is as hard a search as I've ever been part of. I have no idea how this guy is eluding us."

"You have company recently?" Vivien pointed to the teapot.

"Yes, Sherlock. You left me, Viv. I begged you

to stay."

"Since you knew I was coming, Watson, why didn't you put the teapot and one of the wine glasses away?"

"Because I'm not trying to hide anything from you. I've had company. How about you? Maybe you should start, you know…"

"What?"

"Nothing, forget it."

"Dating?"

"You know what I mean."

Vivien didn't want to talk about it any longer and changed the subject.

"This Polk homicide isn't a case for me. I'm not ready."

"What do you want? Ease back? Start with a few light assaults and then on to aggravated when you feel up to it. Problem there is getting the bad guys to accommodate your recovery schedule. Or, you can admit…"

"Don't make it more complicated than it is," Vivien felt her phone vibrating, she had a text. She ignored it. "I'm still scared, Mark, that's all."

"You don't look *scared*. As usual you look like you are totally on top of things."

"I'm terrified."

"If that really is the case then you have to confront the fact that…"

"See, Mark, here is the thing you don't get. Where we are now, today, ten male policemen admit to some sort of 'Post Traumatic Stress Disorder' and they will be heralded for having the courage to admit and confront it. One woman does it and it is proof the entire sex isn't fit for duty."

"I don't think that's true."

"You can't know."

Mark said nothing. Vivien had more to say about the events that had so affected her, which frightened her still. Events that she would never, could never, forget. There were things she wanted to say about herself and Mark, about how she never loved him any less and yet still could not stay with him. About how he'd been unable to help her after what happened with Gary Maher but how that wasn't his fault. About how alone she felt now. But instead, she returned to the case.

"The victim, this Gustave Polk, he was killed by having a tiny ampule of cesium punched under his skin. The chemical reaction turned him into fuel. Lit him up like a torch. He burned to death from the inside out. Who does that, Mark? Who?"

Mark didn't respond. He had no earthly idea. Vivien took out her phone. The text was from her mother.

***

Her mother lived downtown, in a three-story Victorian pile, a row house, attached on both sides. The line of houses was on a steep hill and all gave a sense of having linked arms and dug their heels into the bank to stop from tumbling down it. It was the house in which Vivien had grown up. It was now, with her father gone, two-stories more than her mother needed, or could care for, or afford. Every entreaty from Vivien that Louise sell the place and 'downsize' had been ignored.

The text her mother had sent was a garbled mess, Vivien couldn't make any sense of it. Drunken thumbs all over the screen no doubt. She called and got no answer so judged she should go around and check, just in case her mother was on the floor having a stroke.

Louise wasn't having a medical emergency but another emotional one, was crying when Vivien let herself in. It was clear to Vivien her mother had, as she suspected, put away too much wine. Her supper dishes were on the coffee table in the living room. Everywhere there were books, read and unread, open to a page, closed and marked, annotated, dedicated, stacked sideways and on top of one another to make precarious teetering columns. Vivien could smell cigarette smoke though her mother had pretended to have quit and before then promised never to smoke in the house. Vivien worried her mother would fall asleep with a lit cigarette in her hand and burn the place down. And while this might have been the fate her mother deserved, such a blaze would spread to the adjoining houses full of people who, so far as Vivien knew, deserved to live long and happy lives.

"Who asked for this constant stream of new technology, update this, download that, upgrade this." her mother said, and not for the first time. "Most of what they've fixed wasn't broken. It was merely to fool people into believing they had a need and then selling more useless stuff the obsolescence of which was built in. All of it is made by child or prison labour in China you know. Now I read my television is spying on me."

"And what dark secrets will Google learn about you, Mother? That you have been smoking in the house?"

Her mother ignored the question.

"What is the problem that required you using this new technology to contact me in the middle of the night?" asked Vivien.

"I cannot get the remote to work. I just want to watch some predictable British crime drama, like some lonely old woman. What do they say? 'Netflix and die alone?'"

"You know it's 'Netflix and Chill.'"

"Telling a retired person to 'chill' is such an insult."

"Hollywood doesn't care about you, Mom. You are past your best buying years. Lemme see the remote."

Her mother pointed to the device, sitting in the seat of a threadbare armchair into which it had been thrown. Vivien picked it up.

"That is like…it must be twenty years old…this isn't the remote you need."

Her mother flapped her arms and went off to get herself more wine. It took Vivien thirty seconds to locate the device her mother needed between the cushions of the couch. Louise returned from the kitchen with a fresh glass of something French or Italian, the only places she believed made genuine wine. What was the charade of keeping the bottle on the kitchen counter about wondered Vivien, why not park it on the coffee table where it could more readily be available? For whom was her mother pretending the bottle would not be finished before midnight.

"Oh, thank you, darling. I was going to go mad."

"Okay. I'm going home."

"Stay."

"No, I'm going back to my own apartment."

"It seems a ridiculous waste, there's the entire third story of this place for you to live."

"Live here?"

"Why not? Until you find a new man."

"Too Grey Gardens altogether. And who says there will be a 'new man.'"

"Well, if not, what's wrong with Grey Gardens?"

"Goodnight, Mother."

***

It was an impossibly hot and sticky day for St. John's, but it was New Orleans at the same time and once she turned away from Charles and looked back, he was Mark. She had to go into the nearly derelict rowhouse, its livid paint coming off in large flakes that were, she saw on closer examination actually something organic, were, in fact, fish scales. No, feathers. She had to go in because she'd neglected to secure her service weapon, had left her gun loaded on her night table but within it wasn't her bedroom it wasn't her house and again she was tied to the chair and Gary Maher was coming at her with the lit cigarette in his hand. She could smell fuel, she'd pissed herself but with gasoline instead of urine, her clothes were soaked in it. Gary took a last drag and then flicked the lit butt at her. She could see it tumbling, end over end, through the air of the room toward her.

Vivien woke. Safe in her own bed. But alone. She urgently had to pee. Back under the covers she fumbled for her phone but seeing it was 3:32 in the morning wished she hadn't. There was a text message from the superintendent's office summoning her to a meeting first thing in the morning. With any luck she was being taken off the case and sent back to community policing. She was toying with the idea of taking some riding lessons and then putting in for a transfer to the mounted unit. Most of those duties were ceremonial. She'd never been on a horse but liked animals. They'd always had dogs growing up. She rolled over knowing it would take hours for her to get back to sleep and tried to think of horses even as she realized that joining the mounted unit was a ridiculous idea.

June 7, 2019

Knowing she wouldn't be offered anything to drink Vivien brought a takeaway latte with her to Superintendent Devereaux's office.

She couldn't stop herself from smiling at the view of a black man's broad neck that greeted her. Detective Charles Lafayette was seated across from her boss. He stood once he turned and saw her.

"Inspector," he said, holding out a hand for her to shake.

"If I'd known you were coming, I'd have baked a cake. What's up?"

Superintendent Devereaux spoke before Charles had a chance. "New Orleans police want to rule out Henri Polk as a suspect before we release the name of the deceased. Like us, they anticipate a media storm. We have to stay ahead of the messaging, and we are running out of time. Our forces are cooperating in an informal and unofficial capacity at this stage. I ran it by the Chief and that's how he would like things to stay for now."

"And if an heir to the Polk fortune is a suspect it would also greatly complicate the matter of the estate," added Charles.

"I will likely get the medical examiner's final report today or tomorrow so I will have no plausible reason not to inform the press who the victim was, cause of death and so on. So, we have less than twenty-four hours before I have to issue a statement. You have the fugitive priest as cover, it's the media's sole obsession right now but I'm counting on him showing up, dead or alive, within forty-eight hours. If he doesn't some people won't be moving up the ranks in the way they had anticipated."

"I will not get in the way," said Detective Lafayette.

"Please don't." Devereaux turned to Vivien. "Can I assume that Inspector Ellis will be your host and guide?"

"You most certainly can, my partner in the investigation, Inspector Vatcher, has a lot of desk work so you can ride shotgun."

"Alas, I am unarmed."

"As are the general public."

"Canada, hey."

"We have a late night."

"Oh?"

"The last bands go on at three in the morning in this town."

"Inspector Ellis, I'm from New Orleans."

***

Wu De was confident he was many steps ahead of the local police. He would be on a plane to London in possession of his plunder before the cops here even knew they were looking for it. No, there was no reason to suppose they would even know that there was something for which to look, let alone its nature. There would be unsolved crimes people would eventually forget about. It might take years and several careers, but the murders would be filed away until they disappeared into the darkness. A visitor from the United States had died under mysterious circumstances, "remember that?" "Vaguely," would be the answer. The investigators here were out of their depth.

Wu De was more worried there might be other private agents on the trail, but he'd seen no evidence of anyone yet and it was a small place. All the same, he'd thought it would be wise to monitor the officer he had spied searching Polk's rental property in St. John's. Keeping an eye on the police was good practice. There was always a chance, however remote, the tall lady cop might inadvertently lead the way. She was in plain clothes now and, he saw for the first time on this drive-by, in the company of a black man he hadn't seen before. Perhaps she had been reassigned. He drove on. He was closing on his target, the disgraced Catholic Priest, Father Adam Mackay.

***

By the time Vivien had introduced Detective Lafayette to Vatcher and brought him up to speed on what they had learned or deduced there was only time to grab a sandwich for supper. Vivien was taking him back to his hotel via some of the troubled streets that figured in the search for Father Adam Mackay.

"Surely it was the same in Louisiana, oil money bringing its own sort of woe?" she said.

"Like?"

"Professional criminals. We never used to have pros."

"They've long been a fixture in New Orleans and State Government in Baton Rouge pretty continually since reconstruction."

"There wasn't so much violent crime when I started. The stakes have gone up for some reason. Money?"

"Superintendent said something."

"Did she? About me?"

"Only that there had been an incident a few years back and that you had left active duty and then street work. She said she had no choice put you back out here because of staffing issues."

"Correct."

"So, this 'incident?' Were they pros?"

"No," Vivien almost laughed. "No, he was no professional, he was a fucking crazy. Wack job named Gary Maher. Held me hostage for most of a day, 20 hours probably, a stand off."

"Your boss characterized it as *bravery*."

"I thought she only said there was an 'incident?' And she meant *bravado*, not bravery."

"What did you do?"

"He was holding this young boy. I was the negotiator and I swapped myself for the hostage."

"That is brave."

"It's foolhardy and strictly against protocol."

"But there was a child in danger."

"Yep. That was it."

"You got through it."

"That's all."

They drove in silence for a moment.

"I've been frightened ever since. *Nerves* we say here. I have this permanent sense of dread now. I'm just waiting for the next bad thing to happen. I was obliged to do therapy by the force, all paid for, but it didn't do any good."

"Not religious?"

"God, no. Raised by fundamentalist non-believers. My mother says she is an atheist. My father called himself an 'antitheist,' he thought religion for a force for ill in the world. Why do you ask?"

"There are meditation practices I've heard work for trauma. Some people turn to prayer."

"Don't get all American on me now, Charles."

Charles laughed.

"Whatever works, right? Like they say, 'no atheists in foxholes.' I've been under fire in combat and said a few."

"Iraq?"

"Africa. Chad. Niger."

Something about how chilly and clipped Charles' answer was told Vivien not to ask for details. "Maybe that was my problem," she said, "having nothing to say in my foxhole."

Vivien saw that they were on the stretch of the harbourside road where Gerry Vatcher thought he had spotted Father Mackay. There were a couple of hustlers huddled in a dark office building doorway, waiting for trade she supposed.

"This is where Inspector Vatcher thought he saw Mackay."

"A trick?"

"Looking for the man who was going to testify against him seems a better guess."

"And this relates to the Polk homicide how?"

"My current theory, and that's all it is, is that Mackay is, or was, in possession of a collectible coin or coins of some sort that he was selling to your man, Gustave. He was going to offer the money from that sale, or some portion of it, to Freddie Dinn in return for Freddie managing not to show up to testify against him, or even to recant."

"The deal went wrong and…Mackay killed Polk?"

"With an ampule of cesium? Like some Bulgarian spy? No."

"Maybe Mackay gave Polk this supposed coin," said Charles, "Polk met with another perspective buyer who killed him in order to steal it."

"Polk's a collector, why is he selling it?"

"He made all those calls to dealers."

"Perhaps that was to just to determine its market price, or if it was genuine. Maybe he's checking it against the known inventory of that particular coin. Another thing, we have to believe that whoever killed Polk then searched the place where he was staying. Wouldn't have needed to do that if they were already in possession of the coin. Unless

Mackay has left the island with it, the coin is still out there."

"The Coin. With respect, Inspector Ellis, that is still conjecture. What coin, exactly? What sort of value are we talking about? If someone in this, forgive me, small-town-back-of-beyond, was in possession of something that valuable, something worth killing for, surely people would know of its existence."

"With respect, Detective Lafayette, one of the very few things I have learned during my short years of policing is that there is no end of secrets out there."

"You only know they are secrets because they haven't been kept."

"*Small town in the back of beyond*? I can see I'm going to have to show you around, Lafayette. You'll find our backwater more cosmopolitan than you think."

"I always find big cities more parochial than I thought so maybe you're on to something."

Vivien had a thought. She pulled the car over.

"There were no calls to Polk from Newfoundland before he arrived!" Vivien said the very moment the thought occurred to her.

"I'm listening."

"Fuck, how dense am I? Polk discovered the

coin was in Newfoundland and then flew here and went looking for it. Otherwise, he would have been in communication with some here before coming. Someone here, found it and then contacted him? Somehow, he reasoned that Mackay could help him locate it or a person who knew where it was. Gotta find Mackay."

"You and a manhunt."

"They've missed something. Like you say, it's a small town, there are not that many places to hide."

Vivien put the car in gear and pulled away from the curb.

"Let's get you to your hotel."

"Yes, please. It's an exhausting flight here."

"It is. I can come and collect you in the morning."

"Let me walk to the station and meet you. I need it. What time will you get in?"

"Sixish."

"See you then."

"You'll get to meet my ex."

"Oh?"

"Don't worry he's a good cop and a great guy."

They had reached Detective Lafayette's hotel, The Cabot, one of those barebones efficiency places for business travellers who were picking up their own expenses.

"Good night," he said and got out of the car, closing the door gently behind him. Vivien watched him walk away, disappointed that, as they had in New Orleans, they hadn't mixed a little pleasure with the business. But she was tired herself and Charles had been on a couple of long flights to get here. She resolved that tomorrow she would take him to supper somewhere with good local fare.

***

The windows were smashed out long ago and Father Mackay could feel the wind blowing through the building. Such a shame, these were sturdy and true timber frame structures, made back when the church was freely offered the best work from the big Catholic builders.

The beam of his flashlight fell on some animal droppings, a fox or a coyote he supposed.

The bunks were almost undisturbed so well had they been built.

He was shocked to find an old oil lamp that appeared to have a lick of fuel. He tried lighting it. The rope wick caught but poorly, the flame was the wrong colour and it spit and hissed. He put the glass globe on top to discover it was webbed with cracks. The halting flame and the fractured glass resulted in an unpleasant, funhouse effect. He decided to put it out when he heard footsteps in the dark on the far side of the room.

"Freddie?" he asked.

"It's me."

"You found it. You remembered this place."

"I haven't been able to forget it. No matter how hard I try," Freddie said.

"You and the other boys had great times up here."

"I just about pissed myself in fear every time we were loaded onto that goddamn school bus bringing us out here."

"Swimming. The bonfires. All the singing. I don't believe you don't have some fond memories."

There was a long silence.

"You are truly fucking unbelievable. Say what you have to say."

"I want you to drop the charges against me."

"No."

"I'll pay," said Mackay. Freddie did not respond. Mackay continued, "You'll do it for money...won't you? You'll do anything for money, Freddie."

"Fuck you."

"It is a great, great deal of money, Freddie, more than you will have ever seen. Far, far more than whatever some greasy lawyer says you'll get from the church in some settlement that is years and years away. And after the lawyers take their fees, you will be getting a lot less than you think."

"You have nothing, you're just a pathetic pervert on the run from the cops. Wait until they get their hands on you in prison."

"Oh, I have something. I have the very thing."

"A letter from the Pope?"

"I told you stories. I told them to you at night. I told them to you here when you were a boy."

"That's not the part I remember."

"You do! Remember, the stories about a very special coin? St. Brendan's coin."

"You're mad."

"No, no. Come here, look at this."

Mackay held it by its edges between his index finger and thumb so that Freddie could see the face. It was not quite the size of a 25-cent piece, but thicker. Only now did it occur to Mackay that the coin was not tarnished, was as shiny as the day it was minted, further evidence of its divine provenance.

"This coin, Freddie, was minted in the city of Tyre. It's one shekel. It all makes sense when you examine it properly, when you have the time with it. The head, it isn't of a Roman emperor like I thought, no this is a head of Melgart, a Phoenician God. The Hebrews, you see, they would never accept payment of the temple tax in a coin with the image of the Emperor."

"You are insane. You're a lunatic, you've always been a fucking lunatic."

The impudent boy was not doubting him, thought Mackay, but doubting his maker. He spit with rage now, "**This very coin was in the hands of the apostle Peter, you imbecile!**" He tried to gather his composure. "The coin will not tarnish. Think about that."

"Why should I even care?"

"Because people will pay millions of dollars for it."

Freddie's curiosity was now aroused. He took several steps closer to Mackay, his eye's focused on the small, shining disk of silver.

"Who will pay?" Freddie asked.

"Any collector of precious coins in the world would pay all they had to possess this Holy relic. It is the rarest of things, completely unique, the only one of its kind, a tangible connection to the gospel **in one's own hand as it had been in Saint Peter's.**" Mackay felt himself being overcome. He had to control himself. "They are already here, Freddie, they are already in St. John's looking for it."

"You've met them?"

"The situation has become dangerous; a Chinese man has been looking for me. I believe he has come to steal it. The church has betrayed me, he may be working for them. I need time, I need to be able to move freely so that I can find someone trustworthy to act on my behalf."

"What the fuck do you know about betrayal and trust?"

"Do you want me to tell you the story of how Peter found this coin, Freddie. Do you want to hear that story again?"

Freddie was coming closer.

"Do you want to touch it, Freddie?"

June 8, 2019

Vivian hadn't gotten many hours sleep but the few she had were deep and untroubled by nightmares, so she felt refreshed and bright. Charles, she thought, looked rested too. Mark, at whose desk they now sat, had, instead, the look of someone who had spent the night there. Vivien had laid out her theory concerning Adam Mackay's possible connection to the Polk homicide. Unusually Mark seemed pained to keep up. After some consideration, her proposition only made him angry.

"My first response?" he asked Vivien.

"Yes?"

"Is *fuck you*. You think we missed something this fundamental. You think we are that incompetent as investigators?"

"No, I didn't say…"

"And you think your victim…"

"Gustave Polk."

"Polk, contacted Mackay about some mysterious rare coin, the existence of which I see as pure conjecture..."

"I share that view," said Charles. Vivien didn't appreciate Charles sharing this sentiment. Completely without reason she had expected him to simply sit and listen. But he was a cop too.

"You don't know what this coin is, why it is so valuable, where it came from, why Polk would imagine Mackay had any knowledge of it?"

"That's right."

"You think because we missed the phone calls from Polk to Mackay that we've missed something else that will be evident to a better investigator such as yourself?"

"Be serious, Mark."

"Sorry. You're right. Do what you have to, you won't be stepping on my toes. Fill your boots. Talk to the Archbishop, be my guest. You are welcome to look at anything we have, all the evidence. The charges against Mackay go back a ways so mostly it's paper."

Mark rose from his chair, signalling an abrupt end to the meeting.

"One condition," he said. "If you find Mackay place him in custody first, you can talk to him later."

"Fair enough," said Vivien.

Vivien gestured for Charles to go ahead of her as if Mark's office was, in some way, another property they shared until their divorce. Mark had one last thing to say.

"There is some unpleasant stuff in that file. Forcible confinement."

"You told me I'm ready."

***

They were pulling up to the Archbishop's residence just as a stout man, in a heavy wool coat, nearly to his ankles, in charcoal grey, was leaving. He wore a fedora-type hat which was tilted in such a way as to deny a clear view of his face. Vivien saw a beard, dark with grey patches. The man climbed into a Nissan Maxima.

***

The Archbishop was short and doughy. He was pale, whether from a lack of time out of doors or an illness, Vivien could not tell. The whiteness of his skin accentuated the livid bruise on his right temple and an angry red cut on his cheek that Vivien was sure was made by the clawing of a human hand.

The Archbishop's office was probably once rather grand, but time and neglect made it merely gloomy. The walls were of wood panel and one area had been repaired with an obviously imitation material.

The Archbishop gave every signal of not wanting to be cooperative. When Vivien introduced Charles, she wondered if he didn't scowl. He did not shake Charles' hand with any enthusiasm.

"I hope we didn't interrupt," said Vivien.

"Sorry?" said the Archbishop.

"Your previous appointment…"

"A parishioner, nothing serious."

"The reason we are here…"

The Archbishop cut Vivien off with a raised voice.

"I have told the Constabulary all I know on several occasions. I tell them everything, it never changes, yet they come back and have me repeat myself. It is my sincere wish that Father Mackay is apprehended and faces justice. If I knew where he was hiding, I would tell you. I pray for him."

"As a priest he wouldn't have significant financial resources?"

"No, he would not."

"How about his family?"

"They are of modest means. Father worked in a Shipyard in New Brunswick. He has a brother and a sister on the mainland with whom he'd lost contact, otherwise no family. "

"Did he have any heirlooms, some collectible object that might be of value?"

The Archbishop shifted uncomfortably in his seat. The sleeve of his jacket rode up his arm slightly allowing Vivien to see definitive ligature marks, fine and raw, on his wrist. He pulled his sleeve back down.

"Nothing that I know of."

"We only ask because his flight from justice would be costly."

"I have to take your word for it."

"You've recently received some injuries?" It was the first thing Charles had said since they entered the office.

"I fell. "

"From, Your Grace?" Charles countered.

"The top of the stairs. I'm getting on in years and sometimes lose my balance. I'm trying to be more careful."

"The fall is since your first interview with the police?"

"Yes. I appreciate your concern."

"You didn't go to the hospital?"

"My physician saw me here. One of the few tiny perquisites of this office."

Neither Vivien nor Charles said anything, joining in a conspiracy to silence. Archbishop Doyle could not bear it and said,

"Nothing else?'

"No idea," asked Vivien "where Father Mackay could be hiding?"

"None."

***

Walking to the car Charles asked, "You saw?"

"The marks on his wrist? Yes." Vivien felt slightly nauseous. Her steps were unsure. She worried her legs might buckle.

"Tied up?"

"Tortured to extract information."

"By whom?"

"Mackay is my guess."

Charles saw that Vivien was feeling unwell. "Are you okay?" he asked.

"No," they had reached the car and Vivien braced herself with it, finding some stability. She opened the door and climbed in. Pulling on her seatbelt put her right again, something about its grip giving her comfort and support. As they pulled away, she put another proposition to Charles. She could tell he was worried about her and wanted to show she was fine, was thinking clearly, was up to the task.

"Perhaps he did it to himself?" she said.

She saw Charles observing a car on the next block, a burgundy Mercedes sedan, pull from the curb and get quickly, but not too quickly, away. "Like a flagellant?" he answered.

"A...?"

"Or like Opus Dei, mortification of the flesh as penance, that kind of thing."

"Yeah, I guess."

"There would have been a clue on his ring."

"Really?"

"Yes, some kind of symbol, particular type of cross pattern."

"So, you're a Catholic, Charles?"

"Big time. I'm from Louisiana."

"How's your Voodoo?"

"Why? What do you need done?"

Vivien laughed. Charles made her laugh when laughter seemed so unlikely.

"I did notice his ring," she said.

"I knew you would."

"The pattern was like...bars...bars in a window. Or a ladder? Mean anything to you?"

"No."

"I should have gotten the license plate number on that car," Vivien said.

"Of the gentleman that was visiting the Archbishop before we arrived?"

"Yeah."

"JRT 583."

"Look at you, Mr. Policeman."

Vivien felt her cell phone vibrate. It was Inspector Darlene Hyslop, Media Relations. Vivien knew what it meant, they were going to issue a press release stating that the body on the Cuckold's Cove Road five days earlier was that of Gustave Redding Leonoidas Polk, 62, of New Orleans, Louisiana, USA, and that foul play was suspected.

"Hello, Darlene."

***

Vivien was concerned the fluorescent lighting in the small conference room would trigger a migraine, but they needed a large table on which to spread out the documents. Everything seemed relevant, of interest, there was too much of it. Standing, she reached into another bankers box and pulled out a manila file folder at random. It was bloated with old photographs. The first one she looked at featured Mackay in the company of four boys, between 8 and 10 years of age Vivien guessed, at a school sporting event. They were on a playing field somewhere in St. John's, probably the late 1970s or early 80s. Mackay was beaming, the kids all looked apprehensive. Or was Vivien reading that into the expressions on the boys' faces knowing the charges against Mackay. Confirmation bias was one of the worst hazards of a criminal investigation. And even Mackay was supposed to be innocent until proven guilty. The next photo was black and white, a little older, at a Christmas raffle. Mackay was almost a boy himself, but in a cassock, probably a seminarian at the time. Another, Mackay with fellow priests and Christian Brothers somewhere hot and sunny, stone ruins in the background. Rome, she guessed. Another had him on the ice of a local rink, hockey stick in hand, whistle in his mouth, coaching likely.

Charles was seated at the big table, reading something from the files. She placed the file folder of photos on top of a stack he had selected for scrutiny.

"How it used to be," she said.

Charles opened the file and randomly pulled a photo from the middle of the stack.

"For years," Vivien said, "nothing changed in this town, it just got old."

"Not *good old*?"

Charles glanced briefly at the photo and slid it back into the pile. Something caught Vivien's eye.

"That photo?"

Charles pulled it back out. "This one?"

"Yeah," said Vivien. "is that the Archbishop

with Mackay?" Indeed, it was, His Grace and the accused fugitive in happier times. They were standing near to one another against a castle wall, on either side of a primitive relief of female figure. "A mermaid?" she guessed.

"Could be," said Charles. He turned over the photo and read an inscription, in blue ink, on the back "Clonfert 1979. Clonfert hereabouts?"

"No. That's like Ireland or Scotland, no Ireland, of course it's Ireland." Vivien went to put the photo back on the exposed stack and she saw, on the top, another photograph of Mackay with a group of school aged boys. These were a particularly tough looking bunch of kids. There were no smiles and Mackay's jaw was clenched. There was no doubt about the boy on the far left, apart from the others, with eyes full of rage. She knew this boy as a man. This was Gary Maher.

July 22, 2017

There was madness in the way Gary had lashed her to the kitchen chair. He used some rope and his belt, he'd taken the laces out of his boots to tie one wrist and the other wrist he had tied, with surprising effectiveness, using a plastic garbage bag.

She was young, confident.

The house smelled of mould and mice and cat spray. The kitchen opened onto a cramped living area and Gary had his back to her, he was peeking round the curtain, surveying the police cordon outside.

"You've let the boy go," she remembered telling him. "They will take that into account."

But she couldn't be sure he'd heard her.

She asked him, "Is there anybody you want to talk to?"

And he responded, and she knew these were his exact words. "Got nobody."

"A doctor? Do you want to see a doctor?" she asked,

thinking if she mentioned a psychiatrist he might get angry at the suggestion he was mentally ill. But he didn't answer. And that's when she made the mistake, "Do you go to church, Gary? Is there a priest of someone you would like to talk to?"

She remembered that was when he turned from the window and glowered at her and she sensed she'd said something to anger him. He was smoking a cigarette and took a deep draw, she could hear the paper crackle as it burnt, even twelve feet away. He started coming towards her. She remembered how hard her heart began beating, pounding horribly, racing so fast she thought it would burst. She'd never before known that feeling, that physical distress right inside her chest, the pain of pure panic.

Charles tossed a photo on the table in front of her.

"I'd look for Mackay there."

The photo was a fading colour polaroid, almost square, on the wide white edge at the bottom someone had written, *Aug/83* with a fine tipped marker. Here was young Mackay with a group of similarly aged men, standing in front of a wooden bunkhouse in the woods, the construction of which was nearing conclusion. The building was on a hill above a lake visible in the background.

"Vatcher is so good at this," she said.

***

Indeed, when Vatcher arrived he had only to study the photo for seconds before pronouncing,

"It's on the Indian Meal Line."

"You're sure?" said Vivien.

"I've fished in that pond. The Knights of Columbus raised the money to have the camp built. It was mentioned a few times in testimony against a couple of Brothers, so I think they stopped using it. I recall it was in pretty bad shape last I saw it."

Vivien turned to Charles. "It's a twenty-minute drive from here."

"And," Vatcher added, "those plates outside the Archbishop's place this morning?" he checked a sheet of paper he had brought with him, "JRT 583," belong to a rental vehicle picked up two days ago at St. John's airport, no reservation, by one Avi Jacobson, of Paris, France. Business address is Jacobson…" Vatcher struggled with the French pronunciation, "Antiquaire on the Quai Voltaire. Rhymes!"

"He's in the wrong parish," said Charles.

"Jacobson Antiquaire was one of the places Polk's phone was used to call," said Vatcher. "I tracked Jacobson down. He's registered at the Hotel Terra Nova, in a very expensive suite as it was all they had available when he showed up with no reservation."

"That is a lot nicer place than New Orleans P.D. has you, detective."

"New Orleans is broke."

"The Mermaid. Clonfert," said Vatcher pointing to the photograph of the Archbishop and Mackay.

"What about it?" asked Vivien who was already putting on her coat.

"Nothing, I suppose, you know, coincidence."

"But what, Ger?"

"St. Brendan."

"St. Brendan what?"

"St. Brendan the Navigator. Polk was reading a book about him, some academic tome. Was open on his night table and St. Brendan founded the monastery at Clonfert. The Mermaid carving is on the wall of the Cathedral. I've been there." Vatcher turned to Charles. "We Irish discovered Newfoundland before anyone else even knew it was here."

"Maybe it isn't a coin, maybe it's some...religious relic," said Vivien, "To do with St. Brendan."

"We Catholics love it, fingers and toes of dead saints, dried up hearts in gilded boxes, the works."

"The Brendan story," said Charles, "is myth,

no? It's a common story to many cultures, Sinbad the Sailor?"

"Charles," said Vatcher, "the works is very likely a myth, from the Immaculate conception straight on to Vatican II. But it's a *faith*, right?"

"I'm only wondering what sort of relic emerges from an Irish fable that gets its way here, and how?" said Charles.

"The bible at Polk's was open to a particular page, did you see what he was reading?" Vivien asked Vatcher.

"I did not."

"No, of course, why would you."

"Unless the landlord disregarded my explicit instruction the place is how we left it, Viv. I could go over and check."

"Okay, we're off to Summer Camp."

***

The dirt road accessing the old summer camp wasn't in as bad a condition as Vivien feared it might be. It hadn't been kept up, but was driven over enough to keep it from growing in. Vivien spotted the brightly coloured plastic shotgun shell casings along the way so reasoned it was used by rabbit and bird hunters.

A turn on a rise gave them their first view of the old bunkhouse and other buildings.

"Mackay's not going to be armed, is he?" Charles asked.

"No."

"Like to have my gun."

"Sorry Marshall."

"How are you with yours?'

"My sidearm? I've never fired it on-duty. I'm middle of the pack on the range and am always getting reminders that I am behind on practice. I don't know what any of that means if I was faced with a real-life situation requiring my using it."

"Indeed."

"How about you?"

"I dislike firearms but must confess to feeling more confident having one."

"If Mackay is there and resists it will be strong arms I'll need."

"I will do what I can."

They reached the site of the church summer camp, a group of log buildings on top of a hill overlooking a small lake of a deep blue that suggested depths. There were two other cabins besides the big bunkhouse and another roofed-in space, without walls, likely an outdoor eating area. There was evidence of another cabin that had burned down. No structure was left with doors or windows, they were all open to the elements.

Vivien and Charles got out of the vehicle.

"It's not much in the way of shelter," said Charles. "He wouldn't have been able to hide here for long."

Whether it was the conversation in the car, or some sense of danger, Vivien undid the strap securing her weapon in its shoulder holster. "Hello!" she called.

They walked to the bunkhouse. "Hello," she called again. "Royal Newfoundland Constabulary. Anyone there?"

Vivien had reached the open doorway and was about to look inside when Charles pushed her gently aside so that she was looking around the edge of the door like himself. They weren't in New Orleans but he was right, she was being careless and carelessness was a trait she disliked.

"We'll need a warrant. I can call for one."

"What if I thought there was a chance that the fugitive we are looking for was about to destroy evidence?"

"No, won't fly, we can't be specific enough about the evidence."

"Someone *was* in imminent danger? The property has been abandoned."

"Okay," Vivien said. She withdrew her sidearm and let the gun lead her inside. She hadn't taken five steps when she saw the body.

"Someone was in imminent danger."

"Careful," said Charles. Vivien turned and saw him scanning the space for dangers. They both knew, from experience, that the form on the ground was good and dead. There was going to be no effort to resuscitate. Whoever had done the deed was long gone. They stepped closer. The back half of the skull had been bashed in with ferocity. There was a pool of blood, some looked tacky, but it was well on its way to being dry.

"They weren't satisfied to kill him," observed Charles. "They kept striking him."

Vivien squat down to get a look at the corpse's face. It was Father Adam Mackay, his eyes open, his life extinguished.

***

Vivien was leaning against the unmarked police vehicle Mark had driven to the crime scene. She first thought Charles had moved away to give them distance, privacy, but looking at him now, she wondered if he might not simply be taking in the view. The setting, she realized for the first time since arriving, despite what had happened, was beautiful. Mark looked harried and she resisted the urge to take him in her arms and give him a comforting, chaste, even maternal hug.

"Not exactly 'hanging from a beam' as you requested but..."

"Trading up to a homicide, Vivien. Not what I had in mind. "

"I think we are looking for the same person now, Mark."

"And that's not each other?"

"Hey, I'm not the one fucking the boss."

"Sorry?"

"Or have you switched from coffee to tea in the mornings?"

Good thing Mark was a cop thought Vivien because he would have made a terrible criminal. He couldn't even attempt a lie.

"It happened," he said. "We are trying to be discreet. It's a completely fucked-up situation given the working relationship. We don't even know what we are supposed to do. I mean, does one of us leave the force?"

"My lips are sealed. I only hope she didn't assign me to this pear-shaped case because I'm the stunning ex with whom she can never compare sexually."

"You were assigned the case because you were the best she had. You're the only person that has figured out we've been seeing one another. And she and I both work in the same building, one supposedly full of investigators."

"Is it serious, you and Superintendent Peggy?"

"I dunno, yes…not like it was with you, but we're all older, right? It's harder as the years go for me to imagine living alone. But, you know, she has real ambitions, career-wise, that I think come first. So, yeah, I don't know."

"I bet, with this news, you won't be getting any tonight."

***

Wu De had found his vantage point, hidden in the wood, via a country road that led to an unoccupied cabin. He thought now, being tormented by mosquitos and black flies he should have broken into the tumbledown little building to see if he could observe the goings on across the lake through a window. He lifted the binoculars to his eyes. The female cop (Wu now knew she was ranked Inspector and her name was Vivien Ellis) in plain clothes, was leaning against a car talking to a man he could safely assume was another policeman. He judged from body language they were well known to one another and were of the same rank. More police vehicles were arriving. Half an hour earlier Wu De was ready to turn down the road that led to the crime scene when Inspector Ellis had pulled in ahead of him. She had a passenger, probably another cop so he didn't want to chance following her and sorting things out. He panned the binoculars across the site — it was an abandoned camp of some kind — until he came to a tall black man. Wu De pulled the telescopic lenses from his eyes. No, it couldn't be. He looked back again and indeed the big black man was looking back across the lake toward his location. Wu De scolded himself, there must have been a flash of reflection off the lens of the instrument. Getting low to the ground he crept back to his car.

***

Vivien had offered Mark her best current theory, but he seemed to be having trouble processing it.

"Explain this to me again. Mackay had a precious antique coin or religious relic he stole from Gustave Polk?"

"No, Mackay was in possession of the coin and was trying to sell it to Polk."

"So, Mackay didn't kill Polk. Did whoever killed Polk also kill Mackay?"

"Doubtful, whoever killed Polk remains a phantom. Freddie will know who killed Mackay from the blood on his own hands."

"This is so fucked. And you know…"

"What?"

Mark lifted and pointed his chin over Vivien's shoulder. She turned and saw a dour Superintendent Devereaux getting out of a vehicle.

"I won't be getting any tonight."

***

"I would really like to get this," said Charles. He and Vivien we finishing off what had been an exceptional meal at Raymond's, for many, the best restaurant in the small city. Vivien was late calling for a reservation so they ended up at a small table in the bar at the front of the joint and not in the main dining room. Vivien realized she preferred this space; it was easier to disappear and be unheard in the greater noise and crush here.

"No, it doesn't work that way here detective," she said. "I already slipped the waiter my card in case you tried to pay."

"It was a delightful meal. Those were really the tongues of the fish?"

"Cod tongues, yep, and *Britches* the roe sack. Tongues and britches are actually sort of traditional Newfoundland fare. Not presented so beautifully, or course, and fried in rendered pork fat."

"Tongues and britches, *loves it*," Every visitor tried on the local dialects and failed but Charles, in only two days, was a perfect mimic of the one peculiar to St. John's.

"I always tell visitors to stop trying to do the accent, it's always so bad, so faux Irish, but I have to admit, Charles, you have it down."

"Don't hear from many African-Newfound-landers?"

"Noticed our lack of colour, have you?"

"It's pretty white around here."

"Geneticists come to study us; we have so few roots. One fifth of the population is descended from a single woman who made it across the pond in the 1600s. Heard some Smart Aleck once say we weren't a nation but one family nine generations from its shipwreck. It's getting better, some of the foreign students at the university stay, some..." Over Charles' shoulder Vivien saw her mother come into the restaurant. "Speaking of gene pools..."

"Yes?" said Charles.

Now Vivien saw that Louise had spotted her.

"It's my mother and she is coming over to say hello."

Louise was unable to mask her delight in catching her daughter on a date with a tall, handsome stranger. Charles stood and extended his hand. Vivien introduced him.

"Mother, this is Detective Charles Lafayette of The New Orleans Police Department."

"Nice to meet you, Detective Lafayette."

"And you," said Charles." Would you like to join us?"

Louise looked to Vivien and in a glance conveyed that she was sorely tempted to accept Charles's invitation, if only to have some fun with her daughter, make mischief, but would not because she loved her too much to intrude.

"Why thank you…but no, three's a crowd."

"What are you doing here?" Vivien asked.

"What am I doing at a good restaurant? I was going to grab supper at the bar. By myself unless some widower in town on business happened to sit next to me and then I…"

"Please, Mother, we can imagine the rest on our own."

"Don't worry. I'll stroll down to the Merchant Tavern." Louise said before leaning in and putting her hand on Charles arm to take its measure. Vivien thought Louise was terribly handsy with men. "Careful, she has P.T.S.D." Louise told him.

"That will be all, Mother. Enjoy your meal."

Louise followed instructions and turned to leave but spun right back around.

"It's *The Big Easy*, right. New Orleans? They call it that? The Big Easy?"

"Yes ma'am, they do," Charles said and laughed.

Louise winked at him and left. Vivien felt her neck flushing. Since childhood it was her mother's mission in life to embarrass her. She remembered her father telling his wife to knock it off, to leave the girl alone. She knew her mother meant well, thought it was a bit of harmless fun. It was too late for her mother to change. Vivien knew she should learn to live with it.

"You don't choose your parents," she said to Charles.

"She seems like a delightful woman. Both my parents are gone. Cherish what you have."

"You are right, of course. And you know she is the smartest person I know, in a strictly intellectual sense, not emotionally. Emotionally she is, like, twelve years old. She wanted me to be a scholar, like her, and I sometimes wonder if I didn't end up as a cop just to spite her."

"You're a curious person, right? You love a puzzle. Works for you in either endeavour."

"Less chance you'll end being tortured by a psychopath in the Academy."

"Physically tortured, yeah, but…"

He made her laugh again. She wished Charles lived there, in her hometown, near enough that she could call on him when she needed that.

"Ever do anything else?" she asked.

"Professionally? Other than policing? No. Military service."

"Would you like to?"

"Yes, very much so. I'm a history buff, I could spend the rest of my days in study. Not sure how that would pay the bills though. You have doubts about your career, inspector?"

"Yes. I have a stronger and stronger negative response to threat; I mean my heart is just pounding. I can't stand all the families in crisis, it's the job of a Social Worker. And in terms of catching the bad guys I watch the sharks swimming away as we net all the little fish. I think I may have had enough."

"Then get out."

"Like yourself, there's need of a paycheque and what else am I qualified to do? Am I going back to school? Don't see that."

"It might be a vocation more than a job. Some are called."

"I'm not sure I ever heard it."

"You fit to drive me home?"

"I had but two glasses of that bottle."

"Delicious wine," Charles picked up the bottle and read from the label. "*Chablis, Montée de Tonnerre*. Have to remember that." To Vivien's ear his French accent sounded flawless, he sounded exactly like the Parisians she and Mark had encountered on their doomed relationship-saving vacation.

"I let them pick out the wine," Vivien said. "Come on, I'll take you to your hotel, but first I wanna go park."

***

The population was numbingly homogeneous, thought Wu De. The only other Asian faces he'd seen were overwhelming of the age of university students. He was now too old to pass as a student, a cover he'd used frequently in the past. There were Chinese students most anywhere he'd been dispatched, in Budapest, in Sao Paulo, in Los Angeles. Students and among them spies from the Chinese Communist party, their numbers were becoming ridiculous. An agent of Beijing had recognized Wu while he was on a job in Palo Alto, California. Wu made sure the woman vanished, disappeared without a trace. He used to take delight in imagining the recriminations going up the chain of command as the Party would never stop wondering if she had flipped, had traded her knowledge to the CIA for the price of a new life. Now, when he thought of it there was only emptiness. He had no remorse, no pity, no triumph. He felt nothing.

Most of the people he saw here, on this island, were the pasty white of people of English, Irish or Scottish descent. This close to the ocean it was almost never too warm for Wu De to wear a hoodie and ball cap and go about virtually unnoticed. The trick was to not obscure your face, that aroused suspicion, but to keep it half in shadow so that no one would see enough detail to remember it.

He'd determined that the man who killed Mackay and now had the coin was known to frequent a dive called *The El Tico*. Wu De had no plan other than to survey and familiarize himself with the location. If the man was there, he would endeavour to follow him, find out where he lived and then improvise.

He had nearly reached the stairs to the alley off which the bar was located when he noticed, a block and a half ahead, a car parked out of the street lighting, two occupants in the front. Wu De had seen the same make and model among the police vehicles at the camp by the lake. He changed course, crossed the street and took another road out of view of the car.

***

Vivien had found the ideal place to park the car, on the street but out of the light and with a clear view of the stairs of the laneway that led to the El Tico.

"Can I take my seat belt off now?" asked Charles.

"Sure," said Vivien.

They surveyed the streetscape together in silence. Night traffic; revellers and lost souls. A figure was coming down the street towards them wearing a hoodie and a ball cap which made it difficult to see his face.

"What about this guy?" Charles whispered.

"That's definitely not him," said Vivien.

"Demeanour?" said Charles.

"I don't get anything off him."

"That's something isn't it?" Charles said. "He's giving off nothing, no vibes. He's alone on the street at night and there's nothing tentative, no apprehension. Is he dressed to go to the club? No, to work? We get nothing from this guy."

The man crossed the road and then turned up another side street and was gone from view.

"He heard you," Vivien said.

They were quiet again, so quiet Vivien could measure Charles breathing, slower, steadier and deeper than her own. He was physically fit, and she always had dancing nerves, always had hurried breathing.

"You get along well with your ex," he said.

"Have to. For work. But yeah. He is a terrific guy. Really, he is. "

"It's healthy I think," said Charles.

"Is there a current Mrs. Detective Lafayette?"

"No," Charles laughed.

"Didn't think so."

"Why?"

"No ring. Never see you on your cell phone. Marrieds have to continually call one another, *'did you call that man about the smell from the pipes? Did you forget to pay Melissa's piano teacher again? I thought you said you were going to Nova Scotia, not Newfoundland. How would I know where you were going if you never tell me anything?'"*

"True."

"A *former* Mrs. Detective Lafayette."

"There is someone…well, was. Died many years ago. But always with me."

"Is that enough?"

"Sometimes it's hard."

"You have my cell number."

Charles seemed not to have heard this. He was staring, intently out the window, at the street.

"Him?" he asked.

Vivien looked.

"It's Freddie Dinn," she said.

Freddie was moving quickly. No sooner was he in view than he had darted down the stairs heading for the El Tico. Charles was already on the pavement by the time Vivien was unbuckling her seat belt.

***

Vivien had been at the El Tico on two occasions, once on a call after a stabbing there and a second time to make an arrest. Still, she wasn't familiar enough with the layout to move before letting her eyes adjust. Was it even darker in the bar than in the alley outside? There were corners here in complete shadow. It was just enough time for Freddie to spot her and Charles and to quickly ascertain they were cops. He was two paces from a fire exit. He took the steps like he had practice and was gone. Charles reflexes were quick, and he was ahead of Vivien in pursuit, clearing tables and chairs as he went. Freddie had been talking to two men at the bar, who now put themselves in Charles' way. Vivien didn't see how, but Charles swept the first man's legs out from under him seemingly at the same time punching the second man in the neck so that he was gasping for air.

"**Go!**" shouted Charles. The heavy fire exit door hadn't yet swung closed. Vivien gave chase.

***

Freddie was leaving the fire escape stairs. Vivien had him in sight, there was a chance she would catch him. On the ground she lost him but there was only one way Freddie could have gone. She was running without caution; it was dark and she could easily trip in these unlit alleys. She heard a crash ahead, Freddie colliding with an obstacle. She pushed.

***

Glen saw Tony push himself back up off the floor and take a run at the cop, but the big black guy had somehow turned Tony's momentum against him and sent him over a table and into a wall. It at least gave Glen the time pick up a chair and swing it, but the cop saw that coming too and next thing Glen felt a blow to his ear that forced enough air into his head to make it feel like it was about to explode. He couldn't hear anything, but he could feel his jaw dislocating from a thunderous punch and his balls pounded with the point of a shoe. He threw up. The fist again, the bone around his eye broke in several places. Tony was coming to the rescue, but the cop sensed him and swung around and delivered a round house to Tony's chin that knocked him off his feet and sent a fountain of blood skyward. Glen was losing consciousness just as he realized that Tony had bit the top off his own tongue.

***

From his rooftop perch Wu De was greatly entertained by the foot chase. This lady cop, Ellis, was strong, nearly athletic and showed no fear. But the young man knew the alleyways better, had a lead and was running for his life. She was closing for a time but eventually took the one wrong turn that gave her prey his freedom. She'd drawn a side arm from a shoulder holster. She was a small-town cop, Wu De figured she would hesitate too long before firing. He wondered where her new partner was, the big African. The way that man seemed to be staring back across the lake to Wu De's vantage point played on his mind for a time but Wu De finally reasoned that it would have been impossible for anyone to see anything at that distance with the naked eye. There was a risk they'd call in the canine unit to follow the escapee, so Wu De knew he had to move.

***

One of them appeared to have bitten off a large piece of his own tongue, he was on his hands and knees, blood pouring from his mouth like an open tap. Charles could see from the tremors racking the bleeder that he was going into shock. The other one was going in and out of consciousness. Charles picked him up off the floor and put him in a chair. He slapped him. The man's eyes were quickly swelling shut.

"Where will Freddie go?" Charles demanded.

"Where will Freddie go? Tell me or I will make you suffer." The man wasn't responsive. He couldn't hear, his eardrum must have ruptured. Vivien, gasping for air, entered the bar the way she left. She looked at Charles and shook her head to indicate that she had lost Freddie.

***

Vivien was having trouble catching her breath. She had run as hard as she could run but Freddie had evaded her. She was a moment taking in the scene back in the bar. At two points on a circle made by cleared tables and chairs were two severely beaten men. She vaguely recognized the one in a chair, Glen-Somebody-lengthy-criminal-record. She guessed his confederate on the floor with blood pouring from his mouth was a similarly hardened criminal. 'Glen Somebody' had not too long ago been convicted of 'Something with Violence' so could not be long out of prison. The perp on the floor was quaking, clearly going into shock. These were tough, strong, cruel men and Detective Charles Lafayette appeared to have dispatched them without assistance and having only bloodied his hands and torn his shirt. His jacket? He'd obviously peeled it off to have freer movement. She realized she had Charles all wrong, that by virtue of his charm and good humour, his social grace, she had taken him for a gentle soul. But he was a cop from New Orleans and big man.

Charles was looking her in the eye, almost as if he were seeking her forgiveness for something, but he spoke matter-of-factly, "They don't know where Freddie's gone."

Two uniforms entered the bar with their side arms drawn,

"Police!" said Vivien, holding her badge aloft.

***

They pulled up outside Charles's dreary hotel. It seemed wrong to Vivien for him to spend this night in such a soulless place. She wanted to invite him to the couch at her apartment but that seemed laden with all kinds of suggestions she wasn't sure she wanted to make.

"I'm going to have to write tonight up. Those guys have been booked and the uniforms are taking the guy who lost part of his tongue, Tony Hiscock, to the hospital."

"I caught him on the jaw."

"The other guy, Glen Garland, is such a well-known piece of shit that they determined he didn't need medical attention in the hope infection sets in. But he looked like you messed him up pretty good too."

"I'll take full responsibility. I knew I had no authority when I did it. And it was for naught, Freddie got away."

"How are your hands?"

Charles lifted his hands from his lap to better examine them in the light coming in the car windows. Vivien saw that the knuckles on both hands were raw, so he had a boxer's right and left. The knuckle of the index finger on his right hand was swollen and swelling still. Livid bruising was starting to appear on the left hand. She didn't know enough about this man to so quickly confide in him about the investigation and certainly not enough to have him accompany her in the field. What had she been thinking? He showed up at New Orleans airport and she just went with it, with him.

"They won't be brave in the morning," he said, looking at his hands.

"Those two guys you fucked-up in the bar, they are hardened criminal, real villains."

"Yeah?"

"Taking them out like that, for us coppers here in the colonies, it's like a four-person job. Those boys don't tend to go willingly."

"They probably had a few drinks; they weren't so quick."

"That's probably it."

Vivien left enough silence that would tell

Charles that she knew that probably wasn't it at all.

"I was hoping," Vivien continued. "That tomorrow you could track down this Avi Jacobson, the French antiques guy, and talk to him, find out what exactly it is that all these people are willing to die for."

"What are you going to do?"

"I think I know someone who'll know where Freddie hides. And I think we are running out of time."

"I'm sure we are."

"Once Superintendent Devereaux hears about tonight you'll be asked to go home, and I will be disciplined."

"Wouldn't doubt it."

Charles reached to open the car door and winced from the pain of doing so with his ruined paw.

"For fuck sake," said Vivien. "Wait, I'll come around and get the door, then I'm coming in. I want to look you over, see if we are going to take you to a doctor."

***

Vivien got Charles in the door of his hotel room and went to get ice from the machine down the hall. When she returned Charles was in the bathroom having difficulty trying to unbutton his shirt.

"You use those hands like hammers," she said, "and that's what they become."

She laid the bucket of ice near the sink and took over unbuttoning Charles's shirt. Up close she could see the white fabric had dozens of tiny blood stains. It had been sprayed. She could see into the room, it was sparce, but clean. Dresser, wall mounted television, night tables framing a king-sized bed. He had brought with him a single small suitcase.

The buttons undone she helped him get the garment off his shoulders. Standing this close he seemed an even bigger man. He was quite muscular, like he went to the gym and she wondered for a moment if he might be gay. But she could usually tell. He winced in pain when his arm came out of the shirt sleeve telling Vivien he had hurt more than his hands. She caught a glimpse of a scar on his lower back, a dense dark circle on his brown skin. He was wearing a small gold medal on a chain around his neck. She lifted it from his chest to look more closely. Enclosed in a circle were two old keys crossed to make an X and running straight up between them was a sword.

"What's this?" she asked.

"Was my father's," he said.

"What does the symbol mean?"

She felt his hand under her chin, gently tilting her hand back so that her eyes met his. She felt his other hand now, in the small of her back, drawing her in to him. She felt his lips meeting hers and his tongue against her tongue.

Any self-consciousness she had about her scars were swept away by the irresistible force of passion. They were on the hotel room bed before rational thoughts could enter her mind. It was thrilling to feel him full and hard as iron in her hand. He was starving for her, his mouth all over her until he could stand it no longer, his ruined hands pushed her shoulders down against the mattress and he put himself between her open legs.

As he was coming, he cried out, "No!" He lay on her, still inside. He was suppressing sobs.

June 9, 2019

After a third bout of lovemaking Vivien had fallen into a profound sleep from which she awoke alone in Charles's featureless hotel room. It was just after seven in the morning, later than she had slept in years. Charles was gone. She checked her phone to see if he'd sent her a text. There was nothing. She called him but got voicemail. He was probably talking to that Jacobson character.

What had she done? Girl needed some goddamn impulse control. She'd spent the night with a cop from New Orleans she barely knew! With a professional associate, a fellow law enforcement official with whom she was conducting a murder investigation, an American police detective who had gotten off his leash the night before, seriously assaulting two local villains and likely landing her in the shit.

And why did she feel guilty, like she was cheating on Mark whom she was soon to divorce, who himself was sleeping with their boss? Where the fuck was Charles? Maybe he saw how badly she needed the rest and decided to let her continue in her dreams.

She realized now how in need of human touch she had been. It had been months since even a hand had been laid on her.

She got out of bed and walked for the bathroom. She was a little sore. Charles's suitcase was resting across the arms of the one chair in the room. Since the bastard had slipped out without a goodbye, she felt perfectly entitled to open it. Three plain dress shirts still in the packaging in which they were purchased. Socks and underwear similarly straight from the shop. She lifted the shirts to look underneath. There was a small book. She picked it up. *Precationes Christianae*. The text was entirely in Latin. Poems she guessed. No, prayers. What the fuck? She didn't have time to contemplate any of this, or any of what had happened last night, she had an appointment for which she could not be late.

***

The prison was, unusually, situated near the center of the city, on the side of a lake, on the way to the road on which Gustave's Polk's body had been found. Reformers decried the penitentiary as 'Dickensian' usually unaware that they were speaking literally as well as figuratively as it was actually built during Charles Dickens' lifetime. It was in unacceptably poor condition, even for a prison. Everyone, the staff, the Government, The John Howard Society agreed that it should have been replaced decades ago.

The guards knew Vivien better than they knew most cops because they knew of Gary Maher and what he had done to her. Gary was still here, more than two years after Vivien and he spent their long hours together, and not in another higher security facility on the Canadian mainland because his numerous criminal charges, appeals and psychiatric assessments and reassessments were still winding their way through the system. That Vivien now wanted to talk to Gary seemed strange to prison officials, but she told them that it related to a current investigation, so they obliged.

Vivien would meet Gary through plexiglass so heavy it clouded and distorted the world on the other side. Everything on the prisoner's side of the barrier looked milky. When he was brought into the room, she saw that imprisonment, hard on even the hardest, would soon kill Gary. As he was being led to his seat by the guard, she thought he was in leg irons but soon realized that a short stride shuffle was now his natural gait. Gary sat heavily and looked at her. He had an old bruise near his eye, red marks and a new bruise on his neck. Abuse was doubtless being heaped on him by fellow prisoners and guards alike. He was very pale, undernourished, declining his daily stroll in the yard, preferring to cower in his cell. He did nothing to avert her gaze, he looked straight back at her.

"You remember me, Gary?"

Gary seemed to be giving the question deep consideration. Maybe, thought Vivien, he didn't remember her at all, maybe the event was inconsequential in his universe, maybe he lived in the moment only or maybe in the far past, when he was a boy in the care of the likes of Father Mackay.

"I do," he said finally.

"I am not here to…to talk about what happened between you and I. I'm not here to torment you."

"Sure."

"But I need you to help me help a friend of yours."

Gary nodded weakly. Vivien wasn't confident the gesture meant he was agreeing to be of assistance.

"You remember Freddie Dinn?"

"I do. I remember him."

"I'm worried he is going to come to harm if I don't speak to him."

Tears started streaming down Gary's cheeks, pouring onto his shirt.

"I'm sorry, Miss, about what I done to you."

"Then help me, Gary. Help me find, Freddie."

"Do you forgive me?"

Did she? Would she say she forgave Gary, even if she did not, in order to get the information she needed? No, she resolved that would be a great wrong. If she was going to forgive Gary for the pain he had caused her, pain she felt still, for the scars on her body, it could not be anything but genuine mercy. And she was unsure she had that sort of forgiveness in her. She could not answer for a long time and with every second he was made to wait for it, Gary cried harder.

"Yes," she said. "I forgive you, Gary."

A quake of relief ran through Gary, his shoulders dropped and for a fleeting moment he seemed to find some peace. Vivien waited to feel something herself, an unburdening. But she did not. She was silly to expect it. Her years as a cop had taught her there was no such thing as closure.

"There's this old house, owned by that Blake fellow from Labrador, just out of town, falling down..." he started.

***

Vivien was dialing even as she sprinted from the prison gates back to her car. Gerry Vatcher answered, out of breath, as if he too had been running.

"Gerry!"

"Viv, Christ."

"I cannot raise Charles Lafayette."

"From the dead?"

"What?"

"After the press release, we got a call from New Orleans Police. Detective Charles Lafayette died seven years ago."

Vivien stopped in her tracks.

"You are going to have to tell me that again, Gerry."

"Whoever that guy is, he is not Detective Charles Lafayette. He is an imposter. Nobody at New Orleans PD contacted us before this morning,"

Of course, he was an imposter thought, Vivien, he'd made love to her the night before, he had an uncanny ability to make her laugh, he could take out two of the town's worst villains single-handed, he was gracious and handsome and smart. He could not be real. He was after the same thing Gustave Polk was after and that was something of such incredible value that people would easily kill for it. This object was so precious, so mysterious it was sought after by unreal men, conjurers who appeared out of nowhere, out of vapour. Gerry was still talking but she hadn't been listening. There was a roar in her ears, the din of humiliation.

"I'm just back from the place Polk was renting."

A torrent of thoughts ran through Vivien's head, she was going back and trying to remember, replay things that had happened, all to see how she been duped by the man who called himself Charles Lafayette. Thank God Devereaux had given her the number and told her New Orleans police had called, this was on her and not Vivien. But Charles hadn't fucked her boss, he'd fucked her. She couldn't remember why Gerry Vatcher was going back to Polk's rental property.

"Yeah, what's the story, Ger?" she asked. Vivien felt as if she was going to throw up.

"Both bibles open to the same passages. One is marked. It's incredible," said Gerry. Vivien remembered the prayer book in Charles's monastic bag.

"Do you have it in front of you? Can you read it?" Vivien asked.

"Go thou to the sea, and cast a hook, and take up the fish that first cometh up; and when thou hast opened his mouth, that shalt find a shekel;

that take, and give unto them for me and thee."

Vivien tried to process this.

"You don't believe," said Vatcher, "they…they are all looking for *that* coin? A coin that Jesus… actually…"

"I don't believe anything anymore, Ger."

"You have to come in."

"Sorry?"

"Order from Superintedant Devereaux. She's apoplectic, Viv, I mean she is in a fucking rage."

"Gotta a few things I have to handle first."

"Direct order, Viv. I was told."

"I'm going to see if I can track down this supposed Lafayette guy and I got a lead on Freddie from Gary Maher."

"Gary Maher? You were talking to Gary Maher?"

"Had to."

"Come in, Viv. It's an order."

"You know, Ger, I'm probably finished anyway, so what does it matter?"

***

Avi Jacobson was in need of coffee much stronger than they could provide him at the St. John's hotel he had been informed was the city's finest. He had complained, futilely, on two occasions now so was resigned to drinking the tepid brownish water they served with his breakfast. The pastries here were inedible so he switched to a North American bacon and eggs with fried potatoes which satisfied his hunger but later upset his stomach. Both Doctor Girordano and his wife, Virginie, back in Paris told him he must eat more slowly but it was his nature to wolf down his meals. He had taken too large a bite of buttery toast when he saw Wu De take the seat across from his at the table. He swallowed the half-masticated bread with difficulty and clenched his anal sphincter against an urgent urge to shit in-duced by panic. He was terrified of the man not three feet from his chin.

"Wu! Pourquoi est-ce que vous etes ici?"

"Are you acting for Rome, Monsieur Jacob-son?"

Avi supposed Wu had attended a prestigious British boarding school such was the accent of his English speech. In the past they had conversed in French.

"No," Avi replied. "A client in the Gulf, an Arab." Avi noticed that Wu De was in a well-tai-lored charcoal grey suit, was smiling like he and Avi were the best of friends. Avi supposed that Wu could, if he wished to, kill him right then and there and walk calmly from the hotel restaurant before anyone noticed Avi's corpse sitting in a chair with a half-eaten breakfast on the table before it. Such were Wu's skills. It was why he could charge such extravagant fees for his work.

"An Arab? A Muslim?" Wu was incredulous. "What would they want with it?"

"He's their prophet too."

"But not yours?"

"I have none."

"When did we last do business, Avi?"

"It was that obscene Egon Schiele picture. In Karlovy Vary,"

"Yes…I recall. Deliciously filthy painting. I liked it very much."

"You were paid in full."

"Yes, I was."

They said nothing for a moment. Avi was unsuccessful in his attempt to stop his hands from shaking.

"But this matter…" Wu De said, pausing for a moment to survey the room, making Avi wonder if Wu too was scared of something. "…this matter is another order of magnitude."

"If it is the genuine article then…it's…well… yes. Another order of magnitude."

"Why here? Why in this nowhere?"

"Far from Rome?" offered Avi.

"Perhaps that's it," said Wu De. "You understand, Avi, that I shall henceforth be handling this on my own. I've a commission."

"By interests in Hong Kong?" Avi knew immediately he should not dared have asked.

"You should have reasoned with Gustave Polk imprudently making inquiries everywhere, calling dealers in Zurich and London and Paris, that word would get out. Why do you suppose he was so foolish?"

"To ascertain what it would command in the market before he purchased it?"

"But were such a thing real, Polk would never part with it," said Wu.

"For Polk, all the more reason to know its worth."

"I think you have it right there, Avi. That is a most compelling theory. In any event Polk spoke too soon, he was not in possession of the coin when he made the inquiries. What do they call it when someone comes too soon? Ejaculation précoce?"

"Premature ejaculation."

"That's it, he got over excited. So, Avi, I think you will have to be on your way, back to Paris, empty-handed but at least with hands."

"Believe me, Wu, if I had known you were here, I would never have come."

"Ahhh, you dislike me that much, Avi?"

"It's another order of magnitude."

***

Glen Garland was watching his go-to chubby redhead porn, a new one he hadn't seen before and it was good, hot girl taking a pounding, just about eating a giant cock and yet nothing stirred in him. That spade cop had so fucked him up that he couldn't get hard. Both his eyes were black, one was only now barely open. His mouth was so smashed that he had to take care to place his cigarette on a particular patch of unbroken lip. Glen could take it, he'd been down this road before, knew how to take the time to mend before getting back in the shape to settle some scores. Rick said he would be by with serious pain relief, but that guy was always late, sometimes by days. Three days on the couch, watching the tube, nodding off, that was the ticket. He had broken ribs that would take longer to heal and make coughing and taking a shit painful. He came out of the racket better than Tony who was still in hospital after losing part of his tongue. First time either of them had seen that fucking cop. He needed a beer. Getting off the couch he felt where he'd been hit in the stomach. Cocksucker cop would pay, it might take years, but Glen would make him pay.

Opening the fridge, he thought he heard something in the downtown house's tiny backyard. There was only room for an oil tank and a few garbage cans back there. He went to the small window in the backdoor to take a look.

The hand that came through the window was holding a brick. Glen felt a bone in his face break and a shard of glass enter his eye. The door itself followed the brick, coming off its hinges and into the room and Glen was projected into the kitchen counter. The big black cop came behind the door. Glen fell to the floor and started trying to crawl. He felt a hot puncture in his back and then another. The cop had grabbed a fork from the counter and was stabbing Glen in the back with it. Glen screamed.

"Where is the coin?" demand the cop.

"I don't know!"

The fork again and now he was being pulled from the floor by his hair.

"Where is Freddie? Where is he?"

***

Vivien scanned the hotel lobby for Charles knowing the odds of finding him there were slight. She saw Avi Jacobson at reception, he was wearing his wool coat, there was a suitcase at his feet. He was checking out. She marched up to him and presented her badge.

"I am a French citizen," said Jacobson.

"You were speaking with my colleague from New Orleans, Detective Lafayette?"

"I have spoken to no such person. I wish to leave. I have a flight to catch."

"No one spoke with you this morning?" asked Vivien. Jacobson's brow was shiny with perspiration. He was shaking. He was terrified of something.

"Please, I have to go. I have done nothing wrong, nothing illegal. I am a French citizen trying to return to my country."

Vivien supposed this was true and knew enough to know that detaining Jacobson would give her nothing. She also knew that if she returned to police headquarters with him in custody, she might very well have the badge she had just flashed stripped from her.

"You came here for the coin?"

"I am a French citizen."

***

Gerry Vatcher knew he should have called Vivien. Called Mark even. Anyone. Knew he shouldn't go out into the lot of police headquarters by himself, knew he should be arresting this guy. But when the man he'd known as Charles Lafayette phoned and said that he knew Gerry was a good Catholic there was something in his voice that told Gerry that this was a matter beyond the law, or at least beyond the laws that he was sworn to defend as a police officer. He wanted to have faith but had long ago lost it. He went through the rituals because he believed in the way they built and maintained community. But he believed in nothing while behaving as though he did. Then, reading that passage in Gustave Polk's bible it seemed again that it could be true. Could it? The proposition was ridiculous and yet there were bodies piling up, people were willing to die.

Lafayette, or whoever he was, was standing next to the car, an older Crown Vic. He was completely calm though Gerry knew he must have gathered by now that his imposture was known. How calm and collected this guy had been these past few days though he surely knew he was running against a clock.

Gerry stood before him. The man reached into his shirt at the collar and pulled out a medal hanging by a fine chain around his neck. Gerry saw the modest crest and gave the car keys he held in his to the man without a name.

***

Vivien had left the arterial highway for two lanes of good blacktop and then narrower crumbling pavement with towering cliffs and cold ocean on one side and inky bogs on the other. Now she was driving down another country lane with a soggy dirt surface, the sound of intruding branches scraping against the side of the car. Tendrils of fog were reaching through gaps in coastal hills and over the wind-stunted forests.

Now the growth was into the path's edges and tall alders were overhead so that it was nearly a tunnel. The trail ended abruptly at the site of the cabin. There was scarcely enough space to turn a vehicle around and that was occupied by another car, a Malibu. Vivien couldn't risk getting on the radio and calling in the rental plate. She would only have to defy another order and give away her location. She pulled up right to the car's bumper so that Freddie wouldn't be able to get away even if he got back to it.

Even though the dirt road appeared not to have been much used recently there were signs that the cabin was still occasionally occupied. There was wood piled for a stove. There was an old 25-gallon salt beef bucket, probably for bringing water from a well. This was bare bones living, rudimentary shelter, off the grid. This was a place to hide and try to forget.

If she was with an armed partner, she would call for Freddie to come out but alone she was going to have to have her gun trained on him to be sure he did as he was told. She had to let him know she was not there to hurt him but to protect him. From what she was protecting him from she was not entirely sure. Of its profound danger she was certain. She undid her seat belt and opened the car door. As quietly as she could she got out of her vehicle, leaving the door ajar behind her.

She withdrew her pistol from its shoulder holster. She recalled Charles, or whoever he was, asking how she was with the weapon. All these years on the force and she had, mercifully, yet to fire on another human being. Would she, could she shoot Freddie if he was threatening her life? She didn't know.

She raised the gun and held it before her. She walked toward the cabin.

The paint, a conservative Victorian blue with a deranged neon orange-red trim was peeling off in sheets. There was plywood replacing a pane of glass. There was dog shit at the end of the reach of an unfriendly chain tether but no barking, no panting. There was a gas generator outside the building, its cord led to a crack in an open window and inside the shack. The door was open. Vivien stepped to the side and looked within over her pistol. There were no lights on, no radio or television.

Using the short barrel of the gun she opened the door wider. Her heart was pounding so hard she could feel blood rippling her scalp. As quietly as possible she stepped inside and applied the first faint pressure to the trigger. Another step, looking for shadows, anything to indicate movement. She caught herself holding her breath and made herself breathe. There was a trace of smoke in the air, the smell of charred flesh such as met her from Gustave Polk's corpse.

She stepped further inside. There was a small kitchen to her right, a hot plate and wood stove. With one more step she saw the body on the floor of the main living area. Here was Freddie Dinn, a hole the size of a volleyball had been burned into his upper chest, most of his neck was gone and his face singed. Unlike Polk, Freddie had fought the flames consuming him, his hands were charred. Vivien felt her stomach lurching, tasted vomit and swallowed it back.

Was she mad to have come here alone? She'd made the mistake going in to negotiate with Gary Maher when he was holding that boy hostage and now, she had made it again. She would call it in, wait for support and then, returning to headquarters offer Superintendent Devereaux her resignation. She wasn't made for this. She put her gun back in its holster. She headed back to her car.

She climbed inside and, without a thought, with the instinct she taught those school kids, put on her seat belt before she did anything else. It was all the time it took a tall, athletically built Chinese man to open the passenger door and put something with a dull point to her neck.

"You are well acquainted with the damage this device will do to your person. Don't move," he said. "Or you will burn."

He reached across her and swiftly pulled her pistol from its shoulder holster. He drew it back hard against her breast and sat back in the passenger seat, pointing her own gun at her head. He was pocketing the device he had held to her neck. It looked like an expensive fountain pen but with a conical point where the nib should have been. He caught her eyeing it.

"Mightier than the sword," he said as the deadly instrument disappeared from view. "You are a stupid woman! You've put me in an impossible position." Vivien could not place the man's accent; it was British in some way. Was he from Hong Kong? "If you hadn't blocked passage of my car, I would have disabled yours and fled. This would all be behind you and you would have the rest of your life ahead."

"What are you going to do?"

"**Shut-up!**" he screamed so loudly Vivien flinched. "Did I ask you a question? Is this a conversation? You've done this."

He fumed, his breathing was deep and heavy. Vivien could hear that he was getting control of himself.

"Question: Did you tell anyone where you were going?"

"No," answered Vivien.

"**Liar!**" he screamed, smashing the pistol into Vivien's face. She felt her nose busting open.

"Or maybe not" Now he was speaking calmly. "No one can tell if a good liar is telling the truth. So long in the company of thieves and cheats, police learn to lie easily. I cannot believe anything you say."

He sat in silent contemplation. Vivien felt blood running down her throat. She was not frightened. She vowed to herself to kill this man.

"Drive the car," he said.

"I'm not supposed to take a ride with strangers."

He hit her again.

"Drive."

"Why?" said Vivien "So you can take me somewhere and shoot me?"

"I could shoot you here. If you don't want a few extra minutes of life I can do it right now, I can kill you here. Otherwise drive the car."

Vivien put the car in reverse and backed out of the lane leading to the cabin. Once on the road the Chinese man indicated with the pistol in which direction she should continue.

"This was all about the coin?" she asked.

"Shut up," he answered. Vivien could tell he was thinking what to do next. "It is an object, a thing," he said. "People are crazy for them. Haven't you seen them out in the shops? They want them so badly. They are obsessed with things, things, things. And in the special case of a very rare thing, a very special thing they want the thing so badly they are willing to pay all they have. *All*. They are singularly obsessed with ancient and unique things. A stone carving of a dog, an ugly painting, a tiny coin."

They had reached the main road.

"Turn right," said the man. Vivien did as he said.

"How much is the coin worth?" Vivien asked.

"I told you, you were not allowed to ask questions." He laughed. "Valuable enough that it was secreted from Rome to keep it from Pagan raiders. Valuable enough that it seems Irish monks risked an unknown sea when next it was pursued. Valuable enough…"

Vivien was trying to imagine what she might do to attract attention of any passing motorist so that the police would be called. She looked in her rearview mirror and there was car coming behind them. She glanced again a moment later and it was a Crown Vic, gaining on them rapidly, eating up road.

Who was this? Someone was intent on catching up with them. Vatcher? She eased up on the gas so their tail could gain distance. The Chinese man sensed this, "Why are you slowing down?" He turned in his seat and looked out the back window. It took him a moment to make the same calculation as had Vivien. "Faster! Faster!" he shouted. Vivien sped up but did not floor the accelerator.

She took another blow to her face. She was seeing stars, her eyes filling with tears from the pain, she swerved into the opposite lane and then over-correcting brought the speeding car near the limit of the pavement on her side of the road. "*Faster!*" the man screamed. She glanced in the rearview mirror and saw the vehicle in pursuit was nearly at her rear bumper. Suddenly it was overtaking them.

"Fuck you," she told the man. He struck her again. Vivien could hear the roar of the pursuing vehicle's engine over the strain of the one she was steering. The car chasing them was now alongside, she glanced and saw Charles at the wheel.

Her service pistol was in front of her face, obscuring her view of the road. The gun was discharging, firing on Charles. Glass shattered, pelted the side of her head and her neck. She could feel hot powder burning her face, the report deafened her to any sound but a penetrating ringing. She was going to die, and she was unafraid. Gary Maher was a tornado that stripped the earth. All the fallen timber from his storm had filled a river that ran through her and dammed it at the rapids. Vivien could feel the dam breaking and all that was held up behind it was now free and rushing to the sea. The gun fired again and again her face was burned, something was in her eye. She felt the car Charles was driving smash into hers and then there was an explosive wallop to her whole body and then the world churning, the air going all wrong, forces pulling her in two ways at once and then some thunderous collision and then nothing. She was going to die, and she was not afraid. The car was tumbling, end over end.

She came to abruptly; felt perfectly clear-headed and untroubled despite the fact she was hanging upside down in an overturned automobile. Her view out the space once occupied by the windshield was partially blocked by a deflated air bag. She passed out again. When she regained consciousness seconds later it was full and true, with waves of pain. She was hanging upside down in an overturned automobile on a stony patch of barrens. She saw rescue in the form of two legs — Charles she supposed — through the open space that had been the driver's side door window. But he walked on. She cried out but he didn't return. She turned her head to see what had become of her assailant, but he was gone. The Chinese man had been ejected in the crash. She was suspended by her seat belt; the shoulder strap was digging into her neck. She knew she had broken ribs. Raising her right arm to undo the belt she thought she probably had a broken collarbone as well. The belt would not undo, the pressure required to simply push the release button seemed more than she possessed. She made a final effort and the locking mechanism clicked free, dropping her from the seat to the roof. There was something wrong with her neck. She pushed with her feet and her head went through the space where the driver's side window had been. Whatever had happened to her shoulder or collarbone made pulling with her arms unbearably painful, she continued to use her legs and was very soon clear of the vehicle. To her surprise she stood up on the first attempt. She could hear Charles' voice she thought and stumbled toward it. No, the voice was speaking, shouting in Chinese, it could not be Charles. Only now did she realize she was looking at the world through a single eye. Her left eye was blind. She scanned the area. There was Charles, yes it was Charles, and he was yelling at her Chinese captor in a language other than English. Surely, she was hallucinating. She stepped forward. She could hear the sea, the surf pounding the cliffs in the near distance.

The Chinese Man was on the ground on his back, even from a distance Vivien could see that one his legs was horribly twisted and broken. Charles was leaning over him, threatening him, tearing at his clothes, searching him.

"Charles," Vivien tried shouting to him, but the effort caused too much pain in her chest where her ribs were broken. She kept walking toward the two men.

Charles took something, an envelope, from an inside pocket of the Chinese man and stuffed it in his own. He then raised a hand and brought it down hard to the Chinese man's chest, almost as though he we trying to restart the injured man's heart. He stepped back, crossed himself and appeared to be saying a prayer. The Chinese man began to convulse, he howled, something spit from the area Charles had struck and then his entire torso was engulfed in flame. In seconds he ceased moving, his corpse burning as if it were on a pyre. Charles turned and saw Vivien, he walked towards her.

"You killed him," she said.

"He killed Gustave Polk and the young man, Dinn. I know who he is. He has killed others before. He is a mercenary. This was always going to be his end. He knew this. He is an enemy killed in action. I will pray for him."

"You left me in the car."

"I was coming back for you."

"But the thing you put in your pocket, the object you retrieved from that man, that was more important."

"I am a soldier; I was sent on a mission. I follow orders. That is what I do. You are injured, Inspector Ellis, you need medical attention."

"Do you really believe that Jesus Christ told the apostle Peter to pull that coin, that coin in your pocket, from the mouth of a fish?" Vivien said. Her legs were turning to jelly, she was weak. She needed to lie down.

"Someone took the trouble to take it from Judea, rescue it from the sack of Rome, to hide it in a remote Irish monastery."

"And St. Brendan took it across the sea to New-foundland?"

"It was long ago. It was a legend. Until now."

"What if it isn't?"

"Isn't what?"

"Isn't genuine. A holy relic. What if it is just some old fucking coin?"

"Then all the more reason to take it out of circulation. If you haven't guessed I'm in the *faith* business."

"So, you're not police?"

"I am."

"Not for the New Orleans Police Department." Vivien felt herself beginning to shake, she was going into shock.

"No, not the New Orleans Police Department. You need to get to an emergency room. Where are we? I'm going to call…"

Vivien felt herself slipping again, she was dizzy. She was falling. Charles caught her and she lost consciousness.

September 11, 1843

This was his first visit to Cappahayden since being named the priest at Ferryland. After he'd said a mass, he was given a lunch, a delicious stew of fresh fish and potatoes. It was a primitive place that made him miss Dublin. After eating he'd gone to administer last rites to a woman of the village said to be 100 years of age. No one was literate so there was no means of testing this unlikely proposition, no records. She spoke only Irish and the mongrel English spoken by her descendants was laced with Gaelic words and phrases. Her grandchildren were now speaking an English that the priest was hearing up and down the shore, a dialect that had developed here. The old woman, however old, was from Rathmoylan in County Waterford and was not long for this world. When he was done two of the old woman's great-grandchildren, a boy and a girl, maybe nine or ten years old insisted that the priest follow them to see something they had found, a gravesite of 'the priests before time, the old priests.' They told him, as they walked a rocky trail along the coast, that there were priests in this land before their ancestors had settled, priests before any of the villages along the shore existed. Priests that tended only wild animals and engaged in a long battle with evil spirits that dwelled in the woods. He well knew the history of Irish settlement in the area and that the youngsters were mistaken about the priests, but they insisted there was a tomb with bones, so he thought he had better go investigate. His flock all up and down the shore believed in supernatural forces, in fairies and boodarbys. They held all manner of superstition, ones they'd taken with them from Ireland, others they'd nursed on this rocky shore.

The 'tomb' was a small cave and true to the children's word there was a natural stone lintel over the entrance into which had been carved a Celtic Cross, or something like it, a crude cross within a circle. He bade the children show him the bones within, but they would not cross the threshold. To enter he bent deeply. Four paces inside, at the limit of the illumination from the light at the entrance there were indeed the remains of three people. Three complete human skeletons lay side by side as if arranged. They were easily accessible, so the priest wondered how the bones had gone undisturbed by animals. There was a leather pouch, once seemingly tied off with string that had decayed, sitting within the rib cage of the skeleton in the center. The priest reached for it. Within there was a piece of slate with words, in Latin, scratched into its surface, and a coin, which seemed too shiny to be as old as its face would put it. It looked to be a newly struck ancient coin. The priest read the inscription on the slate.

June 14, 2019

Vivien came to in a hospital bed. She was in restraints that prevented her from moving. She demanded to speak to Inspector Vatcher immediately, but they ignored her and gave her something that put her back to sleep. When she next regained consciousness, the nurse informed her that she would be able to see guests the next day. She was no longer restrained. Her collar bone was broken in two places, she had three broken ribs and a fractured wrist. A piece of glass from either the driver's side door window or the windshield had lodged in her left eye and its extraction without her losing sight in the eye was pronounced a miracle. The burns on her face would heal completely. It was too early to say how her broken nose would heal but she should prepare herself for some reconstructive surgery. There had been real concern that damage to her neck could result in paralysis, so she was put under and prevented from moving. Vivien ate a little lime Jell-o, cried, and fell asleep.

June 15, 2019

The next morning, she ate a full breakfast, with coffee. It was terrible coffee and tasted so good she asked for more.

Her first visit was a delegation from the Royal Newfoundland Constabulary. Superintendent Devereaux and Vatcher sat. Mark stood. She started in with her own list of questions but Devereaux jumped in.

"The man that took you at gunpoint, the deceased, was carrying a United States Passport in the name of Grant Lee."

"His idea of a joke I guess," said Vatcher.

"How so?" asked Devereaux.

"Nothing, never mind, go on," said Vatcher.

"There was a Belgian Passport in the name Ho Ruan in his hotel room," said Mark.

"Fingerprints to Interpol told us that he was Wu De, of Macau," said Devereaux.

"Wow," said Vatcher.

"How did you find all this so quickly?"

"You've been here six days. They kept you under the first three. You knew that right?" asked Mark.

"I sort of did and didn't. I never asked. Go on."

"The weapon was seriously damaged in the murder of De. So far, we've determined it was rigged," continued Mark, "to look like a Montegrappa fountain pen, a high-end pen. Where there would have been an ink cartridge there was likely a phial of cesium. Wu De probably had it in his luggage, maybe his jacket pocket, when he came here. Never would have been detected. Who would even guess?"

"One thing we don't understand is how Lafayette, or whoever this guy was, knew to contact you," said Devereaux.

"He didn't contact me," said Vivien. "You said he'd called back."

"Yes?" Devereaux thought for a second. "I assumed someone had contacted New Orleans Police."

"What balls," said Vatcher.

"It gets better," said Mark, "he called in help to the accident and then somehow stole one of the vehicles that arrived on the scene. We found the car at the airport. Security footage puts him in the terminal. Buys a carry-on bag and some tourist swag to fill it. Buys a full fare ticket to Toronto via Halifax, the next departure on the board at the time. He boards the flight, one of only three African American males, the other two are accounted for so it seems he flew as *Mbaye Diallo* of Montreal. Canadian Passport. It's a Senegalese name. There is no such person. Halifax and Toronto security camera footage…nothing. Like the guy jumped out of the plane."

"Who was he?" Devereaux asked Vivien.

"No idea. When we were in New Orleans it was clear he knew the city well. He sounded like everybody else there, had the same accent, perhaps not as heavy as others I heard on the street. And he knew American law, he cited a Supreme Court case about police rights to search garbage. Was he a lawyer? He was trained in hand-to-hand combat of some kind; he singlehandedly beat the living shit out of Glen Garland and Tony Hiscock. He wore a thing around his neck, some symbol, two keys crossed and a sword. He'd been shot once; I saw an exit wound on his back."

Mark flinched.

"Oh yeah," something else came back to Vivien, "…he said he did military service, saw combat."

"Afghanistan? Iraq?" asked Devereaux.

"No..." Vivien tried to remember. "Chad! And...somewhere else."

"So that's like Special Forces, not regular army," said Mark.

"Or he was French," said Vatcher.

All pondered this in silence.

"Inspector Ellis should rest," said Devereaux. "They say you are recovering well but you almost broke your neck. You take whatever leave you require and when you come back you can return to duty in community policing as you requested."

"I'm happy to stay at Major Crimes if that's okay? I'd like to."

Devereaux and Mark looked surprised. "If that's what you want," said Devereaux. "Come on Mark...Inspector Williams..."

Devereaux and Mark made for the door. Vatcher checked his watch. "I'm gonna stick around a couple more minutes."

"Get well, Viv," said Mark, "I'll check back in tomorrow."

Once they were safely out of earshot Vatcher asked, "Why did you keep his secret?"

"What secret?"

"That Lafayette was working for The Church, the Vatican I guess," said Vatcher.

"I didn't know that. Or at least I couldn't ever prove it. He was doing something that he clearly believed in profoundly, in a way I'll never believe in anything. That he might die meant nothing to him. I'm happy to have even witnessed such belief. Why did you keep his secret, Ger?"

"I've been a good Catholic, you know, my whole life. But I have always had doubts. And with my body turning sour, seeing that this beautiful misery doesn't go on forever, the coin lets me believe."

"Perhaps it's only a story, a legend."

"I know it was more than that."

"Did you help him, Ger?"

A nurse entered the room. Vivien thought she had seen this one before. She smiled at Vatcher in a way that told him he should go.

"See you later, Viv. We are all so happy you are going to be okay. Everyone was so worried."

Vatcher left.

The nurse wrapped Vivien's arm in a tight collar to take her blood pressure. "You feeling better?" she asked.

"Yes. Though I am still very sore where the belt went across my neck."

"Better than the alternative. Is there anything I can get you?"

"A stiff drink?"

"Oh…I don't think so."

"Why not?"

"Your bloodwork. You don't know?"

Vivien's mother Louise entered the room clutching a Tupperware container and a bottle of wine.

"Know what?" asked Louise.

"Ms. Ellis might be pregnant."

***

Brother Thierry had just reached security at London Heathrow when he heard his flight called. "Chiamata di sicurezza per Al Italian Flight One quarantatre a Roma-Leonardo Di Vinci. Tutti i passeggeri devono ora essere al sicuro. Security call for Al Italia Flight One forty three to Rome–Leonardo Di Vinci. All passengers must now be at security."

Brother Thierry handed his passport and boarding card to the official, a slight Tamil woman. A large black man, Thierry was routinely subject to extra scrutiny when he wasn't wearing, as he was today, his cassock. She looked at the passport. "Any metal objects on your person, or coins in your pocket?"

Brother Thierry removed the small medal he wore around his neck and placed it in the large grey plastic tray provided. He reached into his pocket and fished out a small handful of coins, some British, some Euros and one singular old coin and placed them on the tray with the medal. He was waved through by another security official, a white man, on the other side of the metal detector. The official gave him a smile that said he was probably a good Catholic.

"That's fine, thank you, Brother," he said.

"Gracie," said Brother Thierry.

Brother Thierry collected his belongings and noticed that there was also among the coins a Canadian quarter. That was sloppy. He would discard it at the first opportunity. He put his medal back on. He tipped up the tray so the coins emptied into his cupped hand and then returned them to his pocket. He proceeded to his gate.

ABOUT THE AUTHOR

Kit Berlin is an international author who divides the year between the west coast of the island of Newfoundland and the Cévennes region of France.

The Devil to Pay is their most recent novel.

PRAISE FOR
THE DEVIL TO PAY

"Berlin cleverly mingles Newfoundland history and mythology into a fast paced, modern day crime novel. Fans of mystery thrillers like Dan Brown's Da Vinci Code won't be disappointed."
Andrew Peacock
NLBA Award-winning author of
Viral, Bifocal, and *Creatures from the Rock*

"Kit Berlin's novel *The Devil to Pay* is a riveting, gritty crime novel. The story will hook you like a fish and then slowly reel you in. I enjoyed the author's style of writing, especially the little bread crumbs that keep you going through the narration and then suddenly comes back to surprise you. Expertly done."
Paul Carberry
International Best-selling author of
Zombies on the Rock, Carcharodon, and *Terror Nova*

"Kit Berlin's *The Devil to Pay* is a fast paced, compelling book that will draw you in and keep you reading until you run out of pages to turn. A well-crafted mystery that spans the shores of Newfoundland and the old money politics of New Orleans, Berlin manages to keep the reader captivated and on the edge of their seat."
Jon Dobbin
Best-selling author of
The Starving, The Broken Spire, and *Slipstreamers*

www.ingramcontent.com/pod-product-compliance
Lightning Source LLC
Chambersburg PA
CBHW012207030726
47494CB00023B/2556